TWO BROKE WITCHES

Copyright © 2023 by Kate Starling

All rights reserved.

The characters and events portrayed in this book are fictitious. Any similarity to real persons, living or dead, is coincidental and not intended by the author.

No part of this publication may be reproduced or transmitted in any form or by any means, electronic or mechanical, including photocopy, recording or any information storage and retrieval system, without permission in writing from the publisher.

ISBN 979-8-8533237-4-2

Printed in the United States of America

10 9 8 7 6 5 4 3 2 1

TWO BROKE WITCHES

A SAPPHIC FANTASY ROMANCE

KATE STARLING

Note for Readers

This book is a fantasy romance set in contemporary times. While the focus is on romantic relationships and plot, it does contain several plot-appropriate Sapphic sex scenes, as well as profanity. The relationships depicted in this book do not contain abuse, manipulation, or any non-consensual behavior.

WITCHY WOMEN

~DELILAH~

Unit 1B seemed like an afterthought in the five-story walk-up on Madison Street, like someone had chopped up a real apartment and put half the pieces back together again, but without a real kitchen, level floors, and weatherproof windows. It wasn't the kind of place any self-respecting death witch in New York City would've put up with, but in Delilah's mind it was exactly the sort of place she deserved–a total dump.

Delilah stepped into her cramped living room, flipping back her hood. As usual, Iris was perched on the saggy loveseat, cooing to a ficus or a fern or something, and as Delilah rushed by the petite, tawny green witch, she saw her raise a slender hand, a greeting Delilah returned with a one of her typical grunts. It was a measly ten feet to Delilah's room with its black walls and veiled windows, the leather-diesel smell of the death witch thick in the air as always. Her phone chimed with an incoming email.

I have an amazing opportunity for you, Delilah Cruz–unleash your true potential at Panopticon!

It was the usual pitch: A truckload of money in exchange for being some corporate vulture's personal death witch. No murdering or maiming of course–that was too gauche for public outreach–but the implication was clear enough, that Delilah would be threatening, frightening, cajoling, and eventually advising a bunch of men in suits on how to "placate" whichever poor bastards they felt were in their way.

No fucking thank you.

Deep down, Delilah knew people like her shouldn't exist. Death witches were abominations, no matter how wealthy or in demand they were, and had her parents actually had an ounce of courage in their money-grubbing bones, they would have abandoned her in the woods the second her skin went ashen and her lips went purple-black. But no, they didn't see a monster in their daughter's pale visage, they saw dollar signs, an alabaster meal ticket to a fat, lazy retirement, and it was their greed that left Delilah living in this limbo space stuck between not wanting to be a tool of destruction and being too afraid to do what her parents failed to.

Another chime, another email: *Delilah, are YOU ready to discover yourself? Gordian is here to help you find your way.*

Deleted. That was seven for the day and Delilah was sure there'd be more. There were *always* more. A normal death witch would've taken one of these gigs, banked mid or even high six figures for a decade, and then started her own business or went on permanent vacation to somewhere dark and quiet. But stubborn, stupid Delilah had managed to find a way to hate who she was *and* be poor doing it. That was why she was in this shitty shoebox of an apartment, with its peeling paint and warped wood doors, stuck rooming with the only green witch in all of New York and still barely managing to make ends meet. *Take that, Mom & Dad,* Delilah thought. *Wherever the hell you are.*

Her green witch roommate Iris wasn't all bad though, that much Delilah had to admit. She paid her share of the rent on time, kept to herself, and made for some pretty lovely eye candy too, even if it was in that boho-chic-smiles-at-trees green witchy way. Still, they were far from friends. Honestly, if not for Coven Hub, Delilah doubted she'd have ever met the little leafy waif and the plant girl would've been spared seeing Delilah's tombstone face every day. Iris could do much, much better all around–that much Delilah was sure. She could get the hell out of this shit city, meet some strapping young gardener or whoever green witches hooked up with, and put all this behind her.

And yet she was still here. That always nagged at Delilah. She didn't want to go through the song and dance of asking Iris why, but the question remained: What was *any* green witch doing wasting their life in the concrete jungle of New York?

Delilah opened up the bottom drawer of her nightstand and took out a beat-up metal flask. She sniffed at whatever was inside–she'd forgotten what she had put in–and took a sip. Weller. Nice. She scrolled through the rest of the mix of job offers and newsletter crap in her email and opened up her social feed, flipping through annoying meme videos and stupid ragebait until she got to a three-minute-long diatribe on witches. A handsome, square-jawed Finance-type looked at the camera and said:

"New York used to be great. America used to be great. But then these witchy women and night dwellers and all the rest of the paras showed up, and all of a sudden the rest of us–the *normal* people–are fucked. How do you compete with these 'people' who can call lighting, talk to fire, can tell what you're thinking and, maybe worst of all, can kill yo–"

Delilah closed the app. She already knew she was a piece of shit. She didn't need some guy on TikTok to tell her. She took another swig from her flask, but it didn't taste as good as the first. How long was she going to keep doing this? How much longer could she stomach being such a loser?

She picked up her phone and did one of her favorite self-hate activities, opening up her phone's selfie mode. And there Delilah was, in all her pale-faced, sharp-featured horribleness. She smiled and frowned and made silly faces, and she hated all of them, unable to see anything but the wicked bitch who everyone thought–and wanted–her to be.

But as she pursed her lips to the side in a motion that she'd secretly cribbed from Iris, she actually liked what she saw. The moment passed quickly and then Delilah's face was back to the stony, ashen mask she was so used to.

There's the ugly girl I know, she thought with a sour laugh.

~IRIS~

Iris stroked the broad, green-yellow leaves of her new philodendron, trying in vain to get him–Philly–to calm down.

"It's not like that," she whispered to the plant as she moved her fingers across the wide spade of one of Philly's leaves. "She's just… busy."

Iris had no idea if Delilah was busy because on any given day, Delilah barely said two words to her. The pair had been begrudging roommates for almost a year now and since then the only real conversation they'd had was about what to do if neighbors started asking who they were. That was because their building was "no paras", a rising trend in New York that banned witches and other paranormals from renting out units, citing vague legalese about tenant risks and property values.

The problem was the best deals in the city were "no paras" rentals and Iris and Delilah were broke. So they'd lied–just a little–to get a place in Manhattan, where both women had thought they would soon find better jobs and move out into their own places.

It hadn't gone that way. Iris didn't know why Delilah was having such a hard time–death witches were the richest witches in NYC, everyone knew that–but Iris was a green witch, a.k.a. a weed witch, plant girl, leaf lady weirdo, and even out in the middle of nowhere, your average green witch was not exactly flush with cash, let alone in New York. But Iris had grown up in the city and had always imagined it would be her forever home. Until her satiny pink petal hair started coming in, anyway.

Iris adjusted her wig. It was long and pink-blonde with chunky bangs, and no one at the Strand seemed to know or care that it wasn't Iris's real hair. She looked down at her fingers. Even though she'd scrubbed them clean, she could still feel the residue from the Strand's endless paperbacks coating her fingertips, the dead smell of paper lingering in her nostrils. Was that smell getting stronger day after day? Iris thought she would get used to it and convinced herself that working for a used bookstore was, in a way, helping to keep trees from being cut down to print new books, but the truth was that it was getting harder and harder for Iris to go into work. She'd already asked for part-time hours and had started wearing a mask indoors, but now that her fingers were beginning to feel constantly caked in paper residue, she wasn't sure how much longer she could put up with it.

Not that she had a whole lot of options. Ever since her green magick had come in, Iris found crowds suffocating, ruling out most entry-level jobs. She wouldn't even have her restocking gig at the Strand if it wasn't for Coven Hub and that was the best they could do–if she wanted to stay in NYC. Outside of the city, there were plenty of options, such as farms, search & rescue, state parks, and loads more, but Iris had met senior green witches and had seen what they became after all that isolation. Most were lonely old spinsters at best, if not outright lunatics who didn't know how to talk to humans anymore, and some were even rumored to set traps for unsuspecting trespassers.

"Come on, let's get you some light," Iris said to Philly, taking the potted philodendron into her room and setting him on the windowsill facing the disused lot across from the back of their building.

She felt something like a pleased sigh from Philly as Iris inched him into the late afternoon sun. Then she fell back on her bed, waving to the creeping vines that covered her walls and ceiling, along with the other three dozen potted plants Iris kept in her room. Down to just six hours a week at the Strand, Iris was running out of savings fast, even in the dinky little apartment she shared with Delilah. Her latest pipedream was social media, where she'd failed to get followers on Instagram, YouTube, *and* TikTok, an impressive feat in its own way, Iris thought. She'd been trying to teach people how to spruce up their apartments with some greenery, but the reception she received was split between people complaining about how hard it was to care for plants and people telling her to take her top off.

"What should I do?" Iris asked her creeping vines.

The vines, as usual, were quiet and moody. Iris knew they would rather be outside and that they bristled at the meager light they took in, but she needed them too much to let them go. They had originally come from her parents' yard, before Nanna Anna had taken her in, and it was the last thing she had left of them. Iris reached out and ran her hand along the vines, the small leaves inching forward to brush her palm as she did.

Through the wall, she heard Delilah snort at something and say, "Oh, please."

Unlike Iris, Delilah was formidable. She was a cinder block wrapped in leather and studded with piercings, a wrecking ball of a woman who could probably stare down the Devil himself. When they first moved in together, Iris was sure the tall, leggy punk queen would be bringing back dates a few times a week, but it never happened; Iris couldn't remember seeing Delilah with *anyone* in their year together, not in the apartment or outside of it. Of course, neither had Iris but that was to be expected–green witches weren't exactly known extroverts. Death witches though, they were wild, insatiable sexpots, or so Iris had been told. Something to do with their proximity to the other side creating a lust for life was the excuse she'd heard.

Then again, maybe that was just witch gossip. There sure was plenty of that for green witches–Iris most certainly did *not* wear leaves in place of underwear–so who knew what was true. But nevertheless, Delilah never seemed t–

"Fuck!" shouted Delilah at the top of her lungs.

That was more than Delilah's usual opining. Iris waited a moment and was just about to ask her roommate if everything was okay when Delilah called out:

"Check your email!"

Iris grabbed her phone and read the subject of the email:

Important Update: Building Ownership Change, Tenants Must Vacate

As Iris's heart raced, she could feel every leaf of every plant in her room turn her way, not knowing what had made the witch so upset but that it was very bad news for all of them.

UNHAPPY HOUR

~DELILAH~

Delilah came clomping out of her room, followed by Iris. The two girls stared wide-eyed at each other.

"We are so screwed," said Delilah. She took a swig from her flask. "So goddamn screwed."

"Did you read the whole email yet?" asked Iris.

Delilah shook her head, her inky black pompadour fauxhawk whipping back and forth.

"Maybe there's something in there…" Iris suggested.

Iris plopped down on the living room's saggy loveseat and Delilah sat next to her, making the cramped sofa sag in Delilah's direction. Her mind was spinning. It had taken months to find this crap apartment and now she was going to have to go through the process all over again. Goddammit! She'd been pulling shifts at thrift stores and dive bars, and while it wasn't much money, she'd been eking by on it. But between moving costs and the unlikely chance she even found a place this cheap again, Delilah was going to have to either start working nights or resign herself to a soul-sucking death witch job. Great, just great.

"What's it say?" Delilah asked, her nerves on edge.

"Oh no, Arthur died."

"Who?"

Iris frowned. "Arthur, our landlord. You know, the guy with the mustache who helped us unload the boxes from the truck?"

"I thought that was the super or something," said Delilah.

"No, and it says here he owned the building for fifty years… wow. He died of a heart attack and the building went to his kids. It looks like they're going to sell it off to a developer to tear down and put up condos instead." Iris twitched her lips to the side, looking like she might cry. "Poor Arthur."

"Poor Arthur? Poor us! We're going to be homeless," said Delilah. "How long do we have?"

Iris scrolled through the email, her eyes bulging, any hint of tears fading away. "Thirty days," she said quietly.

"You've gotta be kidding me," hissed Delilah. She slammed a fist down on the coffee table, rattling some stringy plant that always reminded her of a giant spider in the dark. "These little shits. They inherit an entire apartment building and they sell it off the first chance they get? Don't they care what happens to the people who actually live here?"

"Maybe we can ask Coven Hub for help?"

"Are you kidding? They couldn't help us find *this* apartment," Delilah reminded her. "All their recommendations were way outside our budget." She finished what was left in her flask and then lowered her voice. "Maybe you've forgotten, but we had to lie our way in here."

Iris fidgeted with the gauzy fabric of her floral print dress. "I remember. So, like… what are we going to do?"

Delilah let out a long, frustrated sigh and stood up. "I know what I'm going to do–I'm gonna go drink."

She looked down at Iris, who was still kneading her dress in her hands, eyes fixed on her glowing phone. No matter how long she looked at that email, it wasn't going to change, Delilah knew that. And although Delilah couldn't imagine anyone more boring to go drinking with, it felt wrong to leave the green witch behind to stew over a pending eviction that she couldn't do anything about.

"Come join me," said Delilah before she could regret the offer.

Iris glanced at Delilah through the veil of her pink-blonde hair. "Join you…? Like, out at a bar?"

"Yeah, you've been to a bar… right? I mean, it's cool if you haven't. Honestly I don't even know if you drink. But you can't just stay here. It's even more depressing than usual."

Iris's hazel eyes darted back to her glowing screen as she idly scrolled up and down through the email. "I don't know, I need to think about what I'm going to do…"

"Come on! You can think later. For now, let's go drink and bitch about how messed up this is."

A tight smile spread across Iris's face. "Okay. But I need to get ready first," she said.

"Not for this place you don't," said Delilah. "It's a dive. A total craphole."

"But I want to look nice," said Iris softly. She tucked her hair behind her ear. "I like looking nice."

Delilah rolled her eyes. "Fine, fine, just hurry up okay?"

Iris grabbed her makeup bag out of her room and hurried into the bathroom. Delilah sat back down on the loveseat, the worn cushions giving so much underneath her tall frame it felt like her ass was sitting on the hardwood floor. She sniffed at Iris's lingering perfume. It was a humid kind of smell, like wet jasmine and earthy trees; Delilah wondered if it was perfume at all or if the green witch just smelled that way naturally. Delilah took a quick sniff of her own armpit and wrinkled her nose. It was certainly not the way death witches smelled, like cigarettes and dirt, a smell so strong that the only thing that covered it up was cloying patchouli cologne.

She leaned back on the loveseat and rested one ankle on her knee, folding her arms across her chest. She could work nights, if she had to. She barely slept anyway. Though right now her longest commute was a twenty-minute subway ride. If she had to take a place in the outer boroughs, it'd get a lot worse. That or she'd have to find some new gigs, but she dreaded the idea of going through the whole "why does a death witch want to work at a bar?" bullshit again. Maybe she needed a new line of work, a ditch digger maybe, or a trash collector, something that would *really* give all those "wow, you're a death witch, you must be loaded!' morons something to gasp over.

Iris emerged from the bathroom looking radiant. Her lips were glossy and pink, her cheeks blushed bronze, and her eyes lined in bold, striking white against her dark skin. It was as if she'd stepped out of a patch of fairy woods, her billowing, bright green gauzy dress trailing her like a plume of ethereal mist.

"How do I look?" she asked sheepishly.

"You're gonna stick out like a sore thumb," said Delilah. Then, when Iris frowned, Delilah added: "You look great. Just don't be heartbroken when you see where I'm taking you."

~IRIS~

Sure enough, Delilah's bar was far from glamorous. It was situated on a derelict corner and looked a hundred years old, with a door that had been painted over who knew how many times and garish neon signs hanging in the windows advertising cheap beer. A sign over the door read "Anyway Bar". Iris had followed Delilah there like an eager puppy, letting the death witch stride in front of her so that Iris could take in the woman's confident, unerring strut. She was practically stitched into a pair of torn black denim jeans that hugged her ass and a beat-up motorcycle jacket, her heeled boots clacking on the pockmarked sidewalk as she strode up to the dive like it was her second home.

Before they reached the door, Delilah turned with muted concern on her alabaster face, pale blue eyes searching Iris for any hint of hesitation.

"Listen, before we go in here, there's something you should know about this place…" she said.

Iris peeked in through the window's blinds, able to see a crowd gathered around a horseshoe-shaped bar. The crowd's faces were striped in shadow and neon, some of them laughing loudly, others staring into their glasses in silent contemplation. But they seemed to have two things in common: they were all women and they were all witches. There wasn't a single man in sight.

"Let me guess–it's a witch bar?" asked Iris with a playful smile.

Delilah couldn't help but smile back. "Exactly right," she said. "If any of them give you a hard time, you can just say that you're with me. Not that you're 'with me' with me, but, you know, just to get them to give you some space. Like I said, you're gonna stick out here."

"I'm going to stick out… at a witch bar," said Iris suggestively.

Delilah scoffed. "Alright already, let's go. I think I'm going to enjoy this."

The bar was even more dilapidated on the inside, with rickety chairs, loud music blasting out of tinny speakers, and the air conditioned smell of sweat and heady perfume. Delilah guided Iris towards two seats at the far end of the horseshoe–the "dark side", she called it–and they'd barely sat down before a tatted bartender in a tank top served Delilah a small glass of something brown. Based on how the tattoos shimmered vibrantly even in the dark of the bar, Iris guessed she was an ink witch.

"Hey Del, how's it going?" she asked.

"Bad," said Delilah, swigging her drink.

"So same as usual, eh?"

Delilah pointed at the bartender and then at Iris and then back again. "Ruth, Iris. Iris, Ruth."

Ruth gave Iris a mock salute that showed off the woman's muscular arms. "Be careful with this one," she said, glancing over at Delilah. "She bites."

"Ruth, it's not like that. We're roommates," said Delilah defensively.

"Whatever you say. The customer's always right. What can I get ya, Iris?"

Iris looked for a menu, but there wasn't any. She stared at the bottles lined up on the backbar and then at the beer taps, completely at a loss for what to order. "I don't know, what's good?" she asked awkwardly.

"Jeez, is she even twenty-one Del? You trying to get us shut down?"

"Relax, she's over twenty-one," said Delilah. She took a long sip of her drink.

Ruth cocked a smile at Iris and brazenly looked the green witch up and down. "In that case, welcome to Anyway Bar," she said, winking at her.

"Okay, okay, that's enough," groaned Delilah. "Just get her what I'm having."

The tattooed witch set a rocks glass down in front of Iris and went off to help other witches. Iris took a sniff of the drink. It smelled strong. Very strong.

"Bourbon," said Delilah, as if reading Iris's mind. She held her glass out for a cheers. "To getting fucked over."

Iris clinked her glass against Delilah's and took a sip. The whiskey was hot on her tongue and burned going down, but it was also strangely sweet. As she tried to work the burn out of her mouth, Iris looked over the bar and caught half a dozen witches trying to make eyes with her, all of them dressed down in worn jeans and band tees, not a single one of them without tattoos or piercings of some sort. Were they just put off by Iris's makeup or style? Or could they actually be interested in her?

"So, I have to ask," said Delilah, startling Iris out of her crowd watching. "Why are you here?"

"You brought me here…" Iris said, confused.

"No, not this bar. Why are you in New York? No offense, but green witches usually don't stay in cities for long."

Iris traced her finger along the top of the glass, waiting for the ice to melt and soften her drink. "I was born here. In Brooklyn, actually. Crown Heights."

"Really? No chance your parents have a brownstone they want to rent out for free, huh?" asked Delilah with a chuckle.

"My parents aren't around anymore," said Iris. She stopped waiting for the ice to melt and sipped her whiskey, biting back the burn. She felt its warmth down the back of her neck.

Delilah sighed. "Ah, shit. Sorry, I didn't mean to–"

"It's fine. They haven't been around for a long time. I know it's kind of silly, but in a weird way, I kind of feel like the city raised me after they left, like everything I learned was from being here," Iris said, smiling bitterly to herself. "The idea of leaving it, I don't know… I guess as a last resort, like, okay, but I'd rather stick it out for as long as I can."

"And soon you'll be on the street," said Delilah, draining her drink. As if on cue, Ruth came back around with a fresh one for the death witch. "How much you think they're gonna get for that building? Fifteen million? Twenty? All for something they did nothing to earn. It pisses me off just to think about."

Iris studied Delilah's brooding form over the bar. She was too tall for the chair, making her hunch over, and she was holding her glass to her dark lips like she was kissing it. Maybe it was the two sips of whiskey or the buzz of the dark bar, but Iris let her gaze trail downward, spying Delilah's breasts pushing against her white tee with the large black star across the chest and then her pale, exposed midriff. Iris took a quick, furtive look at the holes in the tops of Delilah's jeans that revealed her ashen thighs and then pulled her eyes away.

"I have a question I have to ask too," Iris said.

"Shoot," said Delilah.

"You bartend, right? And work at a clothing store or something?" asked Iris.

"Thrift store," corrected Delilah. "Was that your question?"

Iris soldiered on: "I've only met a few death witches but, like… they all seemed to have pretty cushy jobs. Great pay, short hours, lots of benefits."

"What's your point?" snapped Delilah.

Iris steadied herself with another sip of her drink, enjoying how the bite of the whiskey distracted her from her nerves. "I just want to know why you're living in a crummy apartment like ours and not somewhere fancy."

"You really wanna know? Because I'm an ugly piece of shit," said Delilah.

"I don't think so," said Iris cautiously. Delilah's look was unique for sure, but Iris didn't find it unappealing.

Delilah snorted. "Every death witch is an ugly piece of shit. You, you go talk to plants or whatever. Ruth draws pictures that are alive. Frost witches cool down nursing homes in the summer, blood witches go on EMT runs and give people transfusion. You know what death witches do? I'll give you a hint, it's right there in the name: we kill shit. Why should I–or any death witch–be rich? What kind of a messed-up world is that?"

Iris didn't know how to respond. She'd heard all about the work death witches did on social media and from the few other witches she had talked to for more than five minutes. Most famously, they were alleged assassins and makers of bioweapons, but even the tame ones were supposedly on retainer for criminal defense firms and hedge funds, doing who knew what to tilt the scales in their benefactor's favor. Iris turned to the side, so that both she and Delilah were sitting shoulder to shoulder, staring idly at the center of the horseshoe bar.

"Well, I know one thing for sure," Iris said. "You aren't ugly."

"Sure, right," murmured Delilah.

Just then, the front door of the bar swung open. A drunk-faced guy in a football jersey leaned in and shouted: "Witch bitches! Come and suck on *this* broomstick!" Then he and his buddies took off down the block, howling and laughing, one of them smashing a beer bottle on the sidewalk.

"Assholes," said Ruth, removing her hand from under the bar where she'd been reaching for something.

"Does that happen a lot?" asked Iris.

"More and more lately. The mayor's race isn't helping."

"They can't really ban paras from NYC, can they? What would

that even mean?" asked Iris, having heard about one candidate's promise to kick out all the paranormals to lower rents and bring jobs back to "real New Yorkers".

"They can do whatever they want, but they won't," said Delilah apathetically. "Or at least they'll have a plan. Make us all get ID cards or work for them or something and kick out everyone who refuses." She pushed her chair out from the bar. "I gotta go take a piss."

When Delilah was gone, Ruth set glasses of water in front of both of them, more for Iris's sake than Delilah's it seemed, and leaned over the bar.

"What in the world is up with her?" she asked. "I mean, Del's always in a mood but this is something else."

"We're getting kicked out of our apartment," said Iris.

"For being witches?" Ruth was shocked.

"No, the whole building's being sold. Everyone's getting kicked out."

"Oh man. New York real estate sucks ass," said Ruth as she rinsed off a couple of pint glasses.

"Is she really always in a mood?" asked Iris.

Ruth nodded. "I worry that's getting worse too. Which now seeing who she lives with, makes no sense to me. I'd be bright and bubbly if I woke up to you in my place every morning."

Iris's cheeks felt hot. "I'm a lot more awkward once you get to know me," she said, looking every which way but at Ruth's round, smiling face and lithe frame. "I do better with plants than people."

"Well, if I ever get hexed into a flower, I hope it's your green thumb I get," teased Ruth, making Iris cheek's feel even hotter.

"Uh, green witches don't hex," said Iris.

Ruth huffed a laugh and left Iris sitting there bashful. Even though the bar's AC was on, Iris was sweating, the air feeling so thick she could've choked on it. She surveyed the bar again and saw the crowd had grown, with not a single seat left around the horseshoe. The throng of punky witches joked and touched each other, giving playful pokes and sultry looks as the buzzy mood washed over them. Iris couldn't remember the last time she was in a room this small with this many people, and the moment she caught herself thinking that she felt dizzy, needing to grab the bartop to shake herself out of it. She gulped down the glass of water Ruth had given her.

She wasn't drunk, she knew that much, but the green witch in her was coming out strong, like there was a voice in her head shouting for her to go out and find an open field or a thicket of trees somewhere. Iris took slow, deep breaths. She hated feeling this way, like her body wasn't under her own control.

I want to be here! she shouted back at that voice in her head. *Leave me alone! I don't want to be in some stupid forest, I want to be in this bar.*

Iris gripped the bartop harder.

"Hey, you okay?" Delilah said. She'd been back for at least a few moments, but Iris hadn't noticed.

"Yeah, just not used to nightlife, I guess," said Iris.

"Hey, if you want I can take you home–"

"No, I'm good," insisted Iris. "Do they have booths or tables or something though? Maybe something not so, like, in the thick of things?"

Delilah offered her arm to Iris, holding out the bend of her elbow like she was offering up a dance.

"Come with me."

WALLFLOWERS

~DELILAH~

With Iris hanging off one arm, Delilah shouldered her way through the crowd. It wasn't hard for her, the witches moving out of the tall, stern-faced woman's way until she'd reached a scratched and peeling leather banquette against the bar's mirrored back wall. She set Iris down first and then sat next to her, more than a little worried that her roommate had overdone it.

"Are you sure you should keep drinking?" Delilah asked her.

"It's not that," said Iris for the third time. "Green witches and crowds don't always mix. It's like feeling the weather change all of a sudden and getting a migraine or a sinus headache. It'll pass…"

"I'll give you some space," said Delilah. She went to scoot down.

"No!" Iris said. After an uncertain moment, she asked: "Can I hold your hand? I mean, like… death witches are cold to the touch, right? I just need to cool off for a moment."

Normally, Delilah would've corrected this–death witches weren't "cold" to the touch, just a bit cooler than others–but given the circumstances, Delilah held out her hand, palm up, allowing Iris to rest her own on top of it. It was prickling with heat. Delilah wrapped her fingers around Iris's small, warm hand and heard the woman heave a sigh of relief.

"That feels good," said Iris.

"Not the usual reaction," Delilah said. "But I guess that's better than a yelp."

Iris leaned her head against Delilah's shoulder. The two of them watched the swell of the crowd as the witches laughed and drank, Ruth turning up the music to give them something to dance to. It was some 90s song Delilah didn't know the name of and it always made her think of that golden period of her life before she'd started showing signs of being a witch. Ruth caught her eye and made a motion to an empty glass, offering Delilah a refill, but she shook her head no.

"Do you ever wish you hadn't been born a witch?" Iris asked, voice barely audible over the music.

"Every damn day," said Delilah.

Iris held Delilah's hand tighter. "Even if it meant you were never born at all?"

"I'm not so sure it would matter if I were here one way or the other," Delilah said, staring at the throng of witches having the time of their lives. It seemed so effortless for them, so easy. Now and again, Delilah thought it could be that easy for her, too–all she had to do was open that dark little door in her heart, the one that would let all the fucks she'd been clinging onto go to make room for being empty and happy.

"I don't believe that. Not for you or for anyone else," said Iris.

"That's because you're naive," said Delilah with a tinge of indulgence and guilt at telling her roommate what she'd been thinking of her this past year.

"So what?" asked Iris. "Maybe the world would be a better place with a little more naivety."

Delilah nudged Iris's leg. "Yes, just what we need–more suckers."

"Not suckers. People who do things for others without caring what people say about them."

Was that a barb directed at Delilah? She couldn't imagine the pink-haired plant whisperer directing a barb at anyone, but damn if it didn't feel like Iris was talking about her.

"How are you feeling?" asked Delilah.

Iris lifted her head off Delilah's shoulder, and when Delilah turned to look at the green witch, she saw Iris's face staring up at her, her white eyeliner glowing in the dark. The green witch's glossy lips looked like candy and as her humid, lush perfume wafted up, Delilah's voice caught in her throat.

"Better," said Iris.

"Oh, good," managed Delilah.

Delilah's neck felt stiff and the hand holding Iris's felt rigid, as if Delilah was suddenly aware of every tiny movement she was making. She felt too big, her clothing too tight, and had she not just gone, she would've said she had to use the bathroom just to have an excuse to tear her eyes away from Iris. But it was Iris who broke eye contact first and looked back towards the bar. Delilah couldn't be sure, but she thought Iris was looking at Ruth.

"Is this, like, your spot?" asked Iris.

Delilah shrugged. "I like it. It's close, drinks are cheap, people mind their own business. Gonna have to find a new spot soon though, I guess…"

Ignoring what Delilah had said, Iris asked another question, this one the sharpest so far: "You hook up with a lot of people from here, don't you?"

That made Delilah laugh harder than she had in a long, long time. She laughed so hard her shoulders shook, making Iris turn her way.

"What?" asked Iris.

"Iris…" Delilah paused, collecting herself with a deep breath. "I haven't kissed anyone in five years."

Iris made a face as if Delilah had just made a joke but then, when she realized Delilah was being serious, she squashed her smile. She hesitated for a moment and then grabbed Delilah's head, pulling the death witch down towards her glossy lips and gave Delilah a deep, long kiss, their lips nesting before Iris let go, looking embarrassed and apologetic.

"I can't believe I just did that," she stammered. "I'm sorry. I… God, I'm so bad with people."

For the first time in five years, Delilah tasted someone else's lips on her own, able to feel Iris's gloss still slick on her mouth. She licked her upper lip tentatively and tasted sweet strawberries, the verdant scent of Iris's perfume stronger than ever. But Delilah wanted *more*. So much more. She pulled the green witch towards her and kissed her back, driving her tongue between the woman's plush lips and moving both hands down to grasp her waist, fingers pressing through Iris's thin, gauzy dress. Iris was intoxicating to Delilah, better than all the booze she'd swigged these past few years at Anyway Bar, and as Delilah wildly kissed the witch, she knocked Iris's head back against the bar's mirrored wall.

"Sorry!" said Delilah. "Are you okay?"

Iris pulled her head away from the wall and the long pink-blonde tresses of her hair caught on a crack in the mirror wall, her hair pulled away to reveal a bed of pink, satiny petal-like hair hidden underneath. In a moment of panic, Iris snatched up the hair–a wig, Delilah now knew–and tried to perch it back on her head. Delilah stopped her.

"You don't need that here," said Delilah, trying her hardest not to upset the green witch.

Iris didn't look so sure.

Delilah took Iris's hand that was holding the wig and lowered it to the bench, uncurling her fingers gently so she'd let it go. Then she took both of Iris's hands in hers, pushing her pale thumbs into Iris's dark palms, and pulled the green witch close, delighted smiles playing on both of their faces.

Before their lips met again, Iris ventured: "It doesn't *seem* like five years since you've kissed someone."

They pressed against each other, tongues meeting and hands exploring each other's bodies. To Delilah's surprise, there was more spice in Iris than she ever would've guessed–the petite green witch almost greedily running her palms over Delilah's thighs, feeling her skin through the tears in her jeans and reaching around to grab her ass. Those same warm, hungry hands went up the back of Delilah's tee and she shuddered at the electric feel of them, not caring how Iris's overeager touch made her shirt ride up against her stomach and breasts, her leather jacket acting like a canopy for their play.

That was the exact sort of thing Delilah would've rolled her eyes at had she been there alone, but now that she was part of it, she didn't give two shits what anyone else thought. She dipped her lips to Iris's sweet-smelling neck and kissed once, twice, and then let her teeth sink into the rich, tawny skin, not hard enough to draw blood but just enough to get a gasp out of Iris. She pulled away and looked at Delilah with mock offense.

"I thought you said you didn't bite," she teased.

"I never said that," said Delilah, grinning. "You need to pay more attention, flower girl."

Iris leaned in close and whispered into Delilah's ear: "I don't like that name." Then she bit Delilah back, her teeth far harder on Delilah's earlobe than Delilah's had been on Iris's neck.

"Ow!" cried Delilah, laughing. "You're going to pay for that."

"Make me," taunted Iris with a gleam in her hazel eyes.

Delilah was happy to comply. She put her hand against Iris's chest, cupping her breast and finding the nipple through her floral-print dress. Tweezing lightly with her fingers, Delilah looked at Iris as she threatened the pinch that would come next, still not sure the green witch wouldn't change her mind and pull away.

"What's this?" asked Delilah in a husky voice as she tenderly grasped Iris's nipple. "A little bud ripe for the plucking?"

Iris fought back a big, wide smile. "Don't," she said.

Delilah began to pinch harder.

"Seriously, don't," said Iris as she squirmed with laughter.

"You'll have to say the magic word."

Kneeling on the bench, Delilah leaned in close and let her body press Iris against the tufted leather backrest. She slid her knee between the green witch's legs and turned her back to the dancing crowd, catching sight of her own face in the mirrored wall. It was like staring at a funhouse reflection, all jutting features and rough angles, but Delilah knew that was no mirror trick–she really looked like that. She snapped out of her buzzy haze and let go of Iris's nipple.

"What's wrong?" asked Iris.

Looking at the pixie-faced, radiant green witch only made Delilah feel worse. What the hell was she doing? Sure, greens were a little hippieish and a little aloof, but at the end of the day they *made things grow*, helping to create life. That was the total opposite of what was expected of Delilah. Yet here she was, corrupting this green witch because she hadn't gotten any ass in five years… and goddamnit did she want Iris's ass. Not that Iris would want her when the music died down and the lights went up–her pale body, her cool skin, her pheromonal odor that hinted death was right around the corner, all of that was never pleasant in the light of day. If anything Delilah was doing Iris a favor by stopping the green witch from experiencing a horror story she'd never live down.

"We should go home," said Delilah, standing up. "It's going to be hell looking for a new place and we both better get started first thing in the morning. Plus, this bar goes to shit after ten." She looked at the time on her phone. It was only 9:15 p.m.

"Uh, okay," said Iris, looking hurt. She followed Delilah's lead as Delilah settled up at the bar and took them out the back exit. They walked back home in silence.

~IRIS~

What had Iris done wrong? She'd replayed the night in her head a hundred times, but couldn't figure it out: they drank, Iris felt overwhelmed, they sat on the bench, they kissed, they played… what had set Delilah off?

Only two things came to mind.

The first was that Delilah hadn't kissed anyone in half a decade and Iris had, when she thought about it, forced Delilah to kiss her. And although it didn't feel like a forced kiss–nor did Iris really think she was physically capable of forcing anyone to do anything they didn't want to, let alone Delilah–it was something to consider, even if Delilah herself kissed her back after.

The second was much more obvious–Iris's wig had come off. Maybe Delilah knew what a green witch's natural hair looked like but knowing and seeing it in person had to be very, very different things. Iris certainly didn't like looking at it and feeling it–had Delilah felt it?–was even worse, like weird satiny flower petals stuck on her scalp. Iris couldn't believe some green witches actually grew their hair out so it was like a bouquet of flowers. Ugh, gross.

Or maybe it was a bunch of little things all together: Iris's panic attack from the crowd, her hair, wanting to be too close, being a naive "sucker". For the handful of women Iris had dated, their breakups usually had something to do with at least one of those, though none of her partners would come out and say it, of course. No, it was always veiled behind some excuse. Either she was "too good-hearted" (stupidly naive), "too introspective" (not good with people), "too unique" (weird looking), "too caring" (clingy), or some other garbage way to not say what they really meant. Deep down though, Iris knew all these issues stemmed from the same root.

She was a green witch and she wasn't meant to be around people.

Tonight was just another bloom from the same tree, the result the same as always. It didn't matter that it was with another witch and it probably wouldn't have mattered even if it was with another green witch. Nope, solitude was Iris's destiny and she sure better get used to it sooner rather than later. Still, there was something about Delilah that made Iris think that maybe, just maybe, things would've been different this time.

Guess not.

Delilah marched up ahead of Iris, making it hard for Iris to keep up in her kitten heels.

"Hey, hold up," said Iris. "I'm not as tall as you, I don't walk as fast."

Delilah slowed down to a painfully slow crawl. "Sorry that my giant monster feet inconvenienced you," she said.

There was something more than Delilah's usual sarcasm in her voice. Something volatile.

"That's not what I meant," said Iris.

"Whatever," mumbled Delilah.

They got to the apartment building on Madison and Delilah searched her pockets for her keys, cursing under her breath.

"We can just use mine," said Iris.

"It's fine, they're right here," Delilah said as she fished her keys out of her back pocket before dropping them. She cursed again and picked them up, opening the front door. She flipped down her hood and held the door open for Iris, not even turning back to look at the other woman. As Iris followed Delilah into their hallway, she'd finally had enough.

"What's your problem?" Iris asked Delilah.

Delilah spun on the chunky heel of her boot and gave an exasperated laugh. "What are you talking about?"

"Your problem. With me." Iris's heart began to race.

"I don't have a problem with you," spat Delilah.

"It sure seems like you have a problem with me. First, you invite me out to some queer witch bar and tell your 'friend' Ruth that you wouldn't touch me with a ten-foot pole–"

"I didn't say tha–"

"–and then twenty minutes later you're making out with me like I'm the last woman on earth–"

"You kissed me!"

"And you kissed me back!" Iris shouted. She realized her entire body was clenched tight and took a tight breath, sighing it out. "I get it, I'm some awkward 'flower girl' in the big bad city and you're a cool, whiskey-drinking death witch."

"Shhh!" whispered Delilah. "This building is no paras, remember?"

Iris slapped her hands against her sides and groaned extra loud to spite Delilah's whispering. "Who cares? We're all getting thrown out in a month anyway. You're a witch, I'm a witch, what does it matter now?"

There was a sharp pain in Iris's head. The hallway spun and she braced herself against the wall, fighting off a stomach-churning wave of nausea.

"Fuck, are you alright?" asked Delilah.

"I'm fine, I just–"

Iris's knees buckled and she crumpled to the hallway floor. Delilah bent down and picked Iris up, putting her over one broad shoulder and opening their apartment door with her free hand, carrying the petite woman like she was no heavier than a bag of groceries. Delilah kicked the door shut behind them.

"My bedroom," said Iris faintly. "Need to be near my…"

The swinging view of the living room hardwood floors changed to her mossy green carpet and then her vine-covered ceiling. Iris reached out for the vines on the wall, but she was too far away, and Delilah gently picked her up and moved her over so that her fingers could brush the small spade-shaped leaves. Even though the feel of the leaves quelled her nausea, Iris could barely stay conscious, keeping her eyes open just long enough to see Delilah looking over her shoulder at her, a sad expression on her face.

SALT IN THE WOUND

~IRIS~

Iris didn't wake up until eleven the next morning. Her headache was gone, but her body was heavy and sluggish. She sat up and saw that her makeup had smeared onto her pillowcase.

"Fantastic," she said, imagining how awful she must look.

All around her bed were her thirty-odd potted plants, including the half-dozen she kept in the living room–all the cacti and spider plants and lilies and orchids–set up as close to her bed as possible with only a narrow path to her closed bedroom door. Delilah. She still couldn't believe she'd made such a scene in the hallway last night like some whiny brat throwing a temper tantrum.

Iris plucked her wig from between her bed and the wall and settled it back on her head. She adjusted it in the mirror, both relieved and a little bit ashamed to see the familiar long pink-blonde locks. As best as she could, she wiped off her smudged makeup, trying to not look like a complete mess before she had to face Delilah again.

But Delilah wasn't home.

In penance, Iris cleaned the apartment, putting her potted plants back, cleaning out the fridge and trash, and scrubbing down the bathroom, even though it was so old that an hour of scrubbing barely made a difference. But it kept Iris's mind off last night and that much was worth scrubbing until her arms felt like they would fall off.

As she was straightening up the living room, Iris noticed Delilah's door was ajar. Normally it was shut tight. She tried to ignore the narrow portal into the death witch's domain but her curiosity grew and grew until it got the better of her. With one eye on the front door–even though it was far, far too early for Delilah to come home–Iris peeked into Delilah's room.

She wasn't sure what she expected. Maybe half-melted crimson candles everywhere and chains hanging from the ceiling and a giant coffin but Delilah's room was remarkably normal. Boring, even. The walls were black and the windows were curtained with bed sheets. A mattress with no frame was on the floor, with a low table next to it, covered with piercings, chunky rings, and books. So many books. Iris took a step inside to get a better look at the titles: *The Stranger, Notes from Underground, One Hundred Years of Solitude, The Bonfire of the Vanities, The Sun Also Rises* and many, many more. Iris recognized some of the titles but the rest were a mystery to her. And apparently, so was Delilah Cruz.

So she's a reader. I wonder if she's ever been to the Strand while I'm working?

Iris heard the apartment door's knob jiggle. She rushed out of Delilah's room, trying to close the door so the same little narrow sliver was showing, and sat down on the couch. She pretended to tend to Carl, her barrel cactus, while she waited for Delilah to come storming in as always. But the door stayed shut. Iris gave it two, then five minutes and then crept over to the door to look out the peephole. No one was there.

Was she hearing things?

"Am I going crazy?" she asked Carl, spritzing him with a spray bottle. The cactus's flower closed and stayed that way for a few moments before blooming again, Carl's version of "No."

"So you heard it too," said Iris, spritzing Carl again along with the other plants on the coffee table. "Weird…"

Iris was about to ask him how Delilah had been acting before she left that morning but remembered all of her plants had been in her room with her. Instead, she made herself some breakfast–nothing leafy, just a scrambled egg with some hard cheese and charcuterie on the side–and practiced her green magick, thanking all of her plants for their care throughout the night and encouraging them to sway and surge and release their "scents", little invisible clouds of organic compounds that could calm, enflame, and muddy the senses of those in their path. One day Iris might be able to make them much more effective than she currently could–especially if she left New York and surrounded herself with nature–but she was in no rush to become one of those plant queens that could make a hedge maze without breaking a sweat.

Before Iris knew it, it was late afternoon. That was how it was with the plants–the time flew by, their very presence providing Iris with enough sustenance that she could skip a meal and not even know it. What broke Iris's concentration was the sound of their apartment door slamming shut and Delilah for the second time in two days shouting "Fuck!" at the top of her lungs.

~DELILAH~

The note was anonymous and printed out on heavyweight paper, stuffed into an envelope with no return address and tucked in between the apartment's doorknob and jamb. It was menacing in its simplicity:

To the "witches" in 1B–

We always knew there was something off about you two. Thanks to your screaming match last night, we now know the truth. It is the belief of the concerned tenants of this building that it is your illegal, unwanted presence here that has caused its sale–perhaps even the demise of our beloved Arthur Kowalczyk–and intend to bring a civil suit against you for the costs we will incur in the upcoming eviction. If you people have a God, you'd better get down on your filthy knees and pray to them for mercy.

You'll be hearing from us.

–The tenants who belong here

Iris peeked out nervously from her room. Delilah was relieved to see her walking around again, even if the sight of her was a punch in the gut.

"What now?" asked Iris as her eyes darted from Delilah's gaping mouth to the sheet of paper she was holding.

"We're being sued," said Delilah. "What? Why? How…?"

Delilah handed Iris the paper. "Because we're witches. They think it's our fault that the building's being sold."

"That's… that's crazy," said Iris as she scanned the anonymous letter, holding it as if the paper was on fire; Delilah had forgotten that Iris had a thing about paper. "We didn't have anything to do with that. No one even knew about us!"

"But we lied. And there's paperwork with our lie on it. I don't know what anyone could actually do with that, but we're under their thumb now." Delilah ran her hands through her fauxhawk.

"I'm going to call Coven Hub," said Iris.

"Let me do that."

"No, I'm feeling better. Rested. Thanks for bringing all my plants in last night, by the way." Iris flashed Delilah a sweet, sorry smile.

"Yeah, no problem," said Delilah, looking away and thanking her lucky stars that Iris didn't mention anything else about last night. "I'm gonna text some people just to get a read on this thing. Let's regroup in a bit?"

Iris nodded and disappeared back into her room; it was bittersweet to see she'd left her door wide open. In a show of good faith–and because she felt wholly responsible for turning a fun night out into a shitshow–Delilah did the same, tapping out texts to anyone she could think of that could provide useful insight. Anyone except the death witches she knew. She wasn't ready to go down that path, already sure that their recommendation would be to go scorched earth on anyone threatening her.

While she waited for replies, she flipped back to a photo she'd snapped of Iris on her bed in the middle of the night, right after Delilah had pushed all of her plants around her bed. When she took it, Delilah had convinced herself it was just to get a record of how Iris looked, in case her condition got worse. But staring at it now and zooming in on Iris's sleeping face, she knew that was only half the reason, the other half making Delilah feel like a teenager with yet another hopeless crush. Steeling herself, Delilah deleted the picture and erased it from her cloud backup, stomping out all temptation to look at it again.

Delilah leaned her head against the wall she shared with Iris and closed her eyes, listening to the green witch's cheery voice through the wall. Though they had signed their lease together, the lie to pose as "regular" people had been Delilah's idea. The two of them had been paired as roommates by Coven Hub after Delilah had rejected every other roommate they'd offered her, able to stomach Iris because she was too kind to call Delilah out on her grumpy, cranky behavior. They'd been looking for a place for months and while this one wasn't glamorous, it was cheap and in a decent location. Delilah had pressured Iris into the lie, promising her the worst that could happen was having to move, but now the whole damn thing had blown up in their faces.

Replies started to come in. They ranged from sympathetic anger to total bewilderment to, most worryingly, a handful of people who assured Delilah she was truly, royally fucked. One sent her a TikTok video of a NYC-based woman with the username "a_human_lawyer" who dedicated herself to providing "normal humans" legal advice for dealing with paranormals. The video was all about housing discrimination, claiming that paras had an innate advantage and should have to pay higher rents and defer affordable properties to everyone else. There were tens of thousands of likes and thousands of comments in support with a disturbing many of them calling for paras to be banned from renting or owning property in NYC altogether.

The video gave Delilah an idea.

She rushed out of her room and into Iris's. When Iris saw her, she put her hand over the speaker of her phone.

"I'm on hold again," she said, her attempt to keep a brave face on wearing thin.

"Forget Coven Hub," said Delilah. "They're not the help we need."

Iris muted the call and continued to hold her ear to one end of the phone. She gave Delilah a confused, curious look.

"Stavros Basil," said Delilah.

"Stavros 'the Basilisk' Basil?" asked a flabbergasted Iris. "The lawyer guy they banned from YouTube?"

Delilah waved away Iris's concern. "That was bullshit. He wasn't turning people to stone through their screens."

"Really?"

"I mean, probably not," said Delilah, trying to remember how that situation had panned out. "But either way he's not gonna turn *us* to stone. He's a para-lawyer."

"I'm sure he's expensive," said Iris.

"For a case like ours? Two broke witches getting sued right when they've been evicted from their homes? I bet you he takes the case pro bono."

Iris set her phone down and raised the volume, the endless hold music chiming on loud enough for Delilah to hear. "And if he doesn't?" she asked.

"Aren't you supposed to be the optimistic one?" Delilah asked back.

Iris gave up on her call. "Stavros Basil… I guess it could work."

"Just you wait," said Delilah. "The Basilisk is going to welcome us with wide open arms."

She sure as hell hoped she was right.

PARA-LEGAL

~DELILAH~

Two days later, they had an appointment with Stavros "the Basilisk" Basil at his hi-rise office off of Columbus Circle. It took a half hour of convincing from Iris to get Delilah to dress up for the occasion but she eventually relented, agreeing to forgo her usual denim-and-T-shirt look in favor of something more professional. But considering the most professional outfit Delilah owned was a black leather pantsuit that looked like it belonged at a dominatrix conference, she had to dig through the new arrivals at Style Revival, her thrift store job, to find something more suitable.

She wound up in a retro-stylish charcoal blazer with big shoulder pads and a matching pencil skirt that looked straight out of 1992, complete with dark nylons that suffocated Delilah's legs and a pair of toe-numbing patent leather pumps.

But the worst of it was the makeup Iris insisted she wear: clear gloss to make her purple-black lips shine, a touch of plum blush, and so much foundation and contouring that Delilah thought her face looked like something out of a comic book.

"I don't know if I should be impressed you know how to make someone look like this or horrified that you think this is actually going to endear the Basilisk to us," Delilah said as they approached the elevators to Stavros's office.

"Stop touching your face, you're going to ruin my hard work," said Iris. She had also dressed herself up, opting for a fitted, satiny emerald green dress with gold buttons that hugged her hourglass curves and a gold-and-pink makeup look that made her eyes seem like they were dusted with glittering amber. Delilah forced herself not to glance at Iris's body in her tight, vibrant dress, keeping her mind focused on how they were going to convince Stavros to help them pro bono.

The Basilisk's office was all glass and marble and gilded furniture, a Brett Easton Ellis interpretation of Louis XIV exuberance. As they waited for Stavros himself, Delilah and Iris were treated to the burning of a candle containing–supposedly–fossilized wood from the Cretaceous period, along with two complimentary pours of a green tea from Kyoto that Iris couldn't bring herself to taste. Delilah was becoming more and more certain Stavros did not work for free.

They didn't have to wait long to see Stavros, who immediately ushered both witches into ochre wingback chairs before he sat down behind his wide, mahogany campaign desk. He sighed. The hulk of a man wore dark sunglasses and kept his long hair in a dust broom ponytail, it now far more salt-and-pepper than when Delilah had first started seeing news stories about him. He was one of those big men who didn't get fat but got broad, and when he put his elbows on his desk and leaned towards the witches, it felt like he was towering above them.

"So, ladies–how can I get you to where you want to be?" he asked in a deep, gravelly voice.

Iris looked at Delilah, but she ignored her, knowing they had to project confidence.

"We're getting fucked, Stav," said Delilah, wishing she was in any other outfit. She pulled at her nylons. "We need to not be getting fucked."

Stavros steepled his fingers. With his dark glasses, who knew if he was looking at Delilah or Iris or the goddamn glass doors behind them, but he was certainly making the moment linger so long that even Delilah was feeling the pressure to break the silence. But she stayed steadfast, knowing that if they folded the Basilisk would take them for two young idiots with no clue what they were doing. Which, of course, they were. She gave him the icy stare that made most people break, but Stavros didn't even flinch.

"I read the notes you sent me," Stavros said, pulling his hands apart to pinch the bridge of his nose. "In my honest opinion, it's not good."

"For a lesser lawyer maybe," said Delilah. "But you're the Basilisk."

Stavros gave them a flat smile. "You follow the news, yes? Keller is gaining lots of momentum. If he wins the election…"

"He's not elected yet, is he?" asked Iris, her angry tone surprising Delilah.

"No, but he represents a growing sentiment against, well, people like us, which means getting empathy when–I'm sorry, ladies–you did indeed lie on your lease is not such an easy task. People already hate us and you gave them a reason to hate you specifically. It doesn't help that you're also together. That's a double whammy for a lot of people."

"We're not together," Delilah quickly said, the suggestion making her feel warm under her wool blazer. If Stavros could've seen Delilah in her natural habitat and not dressed up like a vogue model, he'd have known in an instant there were more than a few things wrong with her that no other girl should have to put up with. She was tempted to give him a taste of that true self but held her tongue, still hoping they could win him over.

Iris raised her hand like a kid in class.

"Yes, dear…?" asked Stavros, disarmed by Iris's politeness.

"Even if they hate us, I don't see how there's any legal basis for a lawsuit. Wouldn't they have to prove we actually did something to cause the sale of the building or to lower its property value?" Iris asked primly, keeping such a straight-backed posture that in that moment the little green witch looked as big as the Basilisk himself. Delilah smiled.

"You've watched too many TV shows, I'm afraid," said Stavros, his chair squeaking as he leaned back. "This is a civil suit, not a criminal case. The burden of proof is much, much lower. A prosecutor in a civil suit only has to show a 'preponderance of evidence', basically convincing a jury that there's just a greater than fifty percent chance their claim is true."

Clouds rolled over the Manhattan sky, blocking out the sun. Stavros continued.

"Now, you two seem like smart young witches so tell me: how likely is it in this political climate that you get enough jurors so empathetic to the para cause that they're willing to deny there's a coin flip chance you did something–intentionally or otherwise– to affect your apartment building's desirability? Seriously, I want to hear from each of you how likely you think that is. Let's start with you, Ms. Cruz."

Delilah shook her head ruefully. "Not very likely."

"And you, Ms. Williams? That is a lovely dress by the way."

"I suppose the odds are against us," said Iris, shoulders sagging with a sigh. "And thank you."

"You both really are dressed impeccably. I liked those shoulder pads, Ms. Cruz. Very vintage. You should see some of the deadbeats that come in here, dressed in old jeans and stained shirts," said Stavros with a chuckle. Seeing that neither of the witches was laughing along with him, Stavros quieted. "Anyway, I wish I had better answers for you, I really do."

"So that's it then?" asked Delilah. "We're just… gonna get sued and probably lose and be in debt for the rest of our lives?"

Stavros tilted his head to one side. "Well, I don't know about the debt part. The market is always looking for DWEs and it pays very, very well for them."

DWEs. Death Witch Employees. Delilah hated that term almost as much as she hated how people pronounced it "dwees". She swallowed her irritation, looking forward to when they were out of that office so she could let out a scream.

"And if you're not a death witch?" asked Iris.

"Ah right, you two aren't together," said Stavros with a gleam in his eye, as if they were all in on some private joke. He scratched his nose.

"I guess I could just go hide in the woods like a good green witch," Iris said bitterly. "I can't be sued if they can't find me. I'm sure I'll wind up alone in the wilderness eventually anyway…"

Delilah winced, thinking back to what Iris had said during their hallway fight: *I'm just a 'flower girl' in the big bad city*. She felt shitty about making out with Iris all over again, no matter how much she had enjoyed it in the moment. It was one thing for Delilah to go and make a mess of her life, it was another to drag Iris down with her. What a classic death witch move–no fun without a little destruction to go along with it.

"Listen," said Stavros. "If you want my non-legal advice, here it is: This civil suit looks like it's coming from some angry neighbors who are probably scared that they're not going to have a place to live in a month. If you can find a way to make these neighbors a little less angry and a little less scared, you might be able to get them to call off the suit altogether. Or even better, figure out a way to stop the sale of the building. Then they'll *really* have no reason to sue you."

"How are we supposed to do that?" asked Delilah.

Stavros shrugged his big shoulders. "Like I said, you two seem like smart young witches. Put your heads together and figure something out. Just whatever you do, don't do anything else to provoke your neighbors. You don't need to give them any more reasons to target you."

When Stavros stood up, Delilah knew their time with him was over. She and Iris followed suit and the large man in the dark sunglasses escorted them to the double glass doors of his office.

"Before we go, one tiny unrelated question," said Delilah.

"Is it about me turning people to stone through their computer screens or whatever?" Stavros asked, raising a bushy eyebrow.

Delilah gave a chaste nod.

"Complete hogwash," said Stavros. "Even if I wanted to, I couldn't do that. But take it as another thing to think about."

"What do you mean?" asked Iris.

"I mean that if I, as a lawyer who bills twelve hundred an hour, can get banned from one of the world's biggest websites for something I can't even do, how do you think you two will fare? Please, take the advice I gave you and figure out a way to get your neighbors to like you. If this election goes south, we paras are going to need all the allies we can get."

With that, Delilah and Iris found themselves back in the Basilisk's reception area, being offered another complimentary pour of tea. Delilah declined for them with no argument from Iris. The two of them were silent on the elevator ride back down, Delilah at a complete loss for how she was going to get anyone to like her when she couldn't even stand herself.

~IRIS~

When they stepped out onto the street, the sun broke through the clouds and Iris bathed her face in its warm light. It centered her and calmed the churning concerns she had from their dud of a meeting with Stavros, allowing her to forget for a few moments that she was facing a lawsuit she couldn't win with no way out but to run or try to get a bunch of strangers who already hated her to like her. Why did everything in life have to come down to how you handled people? School, work, finding an apartment… it was all one big game of whoever could be the most likable and make the most friends, but all Iris wanted was to be alone among the other eight and a half million New Yorkers without having to schmooze and cajole anyone.

Well, maybe not completely alone.

Delilah went to flip up her hood and then realized she wasn't wearing her leather jacket. She squirmed in her tapered blazer and pencil skirt, trying to avoid all eye contact with the droves of people that passed them by on the street. A few paused to stare at the women, but most seemed to be rushing off to some meeting or another.

"That was a waste of time," said Delilah, picking a direction away from the busy intersection nearby. "At least we know how screwed we are now."

"I've never really thought about trying to get people to like me," said Iris. "Plants, sure, but people? I don't even know where to start."

"You're plenty likable. You're peppy, you're fashionable, you're cute." There was a beat of silence between the two women before Delilah continued. "Me though… they're gonna get one look at my face and call for me to be burned at the stake."

Iris opened her mouth to push back on Delilah but stopped. She wanted to tell Delilah that she had a lovely face and if she stopped hiding it all the time behind scowls and grunts, others would see that too. But she didn't want Delilah to take it the wrong way. They'd had their little fling and it hadn't worked out, there was no need to keep making Delilah reject her. Iris could feel rejected all by herself.

They turned the corner and Iris could feel they were slowly heading towards Central Park, the pulse of nature like a pleasant warmth in her chest.

"Maybe we could throw a party," Iris offered.

"Where? In our apartment? People would have to take turns the place is so small," said Delilah, tugging on her blazer. "Plus, a party thrown by some witches… unless it's Halloween, I don't think we're gonna have many takers."

"What about an outdoor party? Like a picnic or a barbeque?"

"Twenty bucks says we do that and one of our 'concerned

neighbors' calls the cops on us for performing satanic rituals in the street."

As the park came into view at the end of the block, Iris could hear a light buzzing in her ears, like tinnitus, only with a vibration that made her teeth ache. She rubbed her temples.

"Well then what are we going to do?" she asked. "No parties, no picnics, nothing public."

Delilah looked down at Iris. "Is it too much if I suggest giving them plants that release happy endorphins or something?"

Iris stared daggers back at the tall witch.

"Okay, okay, no plants," said Delilah. "Probably no gifts at all. How about ideas on how we might keep Arnie's kids from selling the building?"

"*Arthur's* kids," Iris corrected. "Maybe we can just… ask?"

Delilah snorted. "You think they're not going to sell the building if we ask them nicely?"

"Well, no, but like maybe they'll tell us something useful," said Iris.

"Something useful like what?" Delilah faked a dopey voice, imitating a response from Arthur's kids: "Oh, we're selling the building *unless* someone can tell us the difference between a cactus and a succulent."

"A cactus *is* a succulent," said Iris. "And I don't know! I'm just trying to brainstorm here."

The ringing in Iris's ears got worse. She grabbed her head and groaned.

"Oh shit, this again?" asked Delilah. "Come on, let's sit you down."

"No, it's something else," said Iris. As she focused on the piercing sound, it started to sound less and less like a high-pitched ringing and more like something else.

Screaming.

Iris ran up ahead, forcing Delilah to trail after her. She blindly crossed Central Park West, nearly getting hit by a yellow cab, and kicked off her kitten heels so she could climb over the park's stone wall. The second her bare feet touched the grass, Iris could see the source of the screaming–a magnificent, old elm tree five hundred feet away. To everyone else it looked like the other willowy, broad-branching elms in the park, but to Iris it was covered in wild, lavender flame, the "blaze" bigger than their apartment building. She ran towards the tree, not looking to see if Delilah was keeping up with her.

As Iris neared the tree, she saw there were four park workers standing around it. Two were putting up a barrier of yellow caution tape, while two others were readying a chainsaw.

No! thought Iris. *It's still alive, it's healthy! You can't do this!*

The workers shouted at her as she tore through the caution tape and planted herself in front of the tree with her arms spread wide, chest heaving with strained, shallow breaths.

"Lady, what are you doing!" yelled the worker closest to her, a man with sweaty hair and a thick beard.

"You can't cut this tree down," begged Iris.

The workers gave each other bewildered looks. One asked if Iris was on drugs and another looked around, like this was all part of an elaborate prank. The bearded worker set his chainsaw down, approaching Iris with an exhausted sigh.

"Lady, this tree is infested with lanternflies. Just take a look. It's gotta go," he said.

Not trusting that the worker wasn't lying to get her to drop her guard, Iris quickly glanced over her shoulder. Through the swirling, lavender fire-like emanations rolling off the elm's trunk, she could see hundreds of spotted lanternflies, their ladybug-like spotting making it look like the tree's bark was dancing. Still, despite the roiling sea of pests covering the tree's branches, Iris could feel the elm itself was alive and healthy underneath. She grabbed her head in pain.

"Jesus, she's crazy," the worker's partner said, a tall, heavyset guy in dark green overalls.

"I'm not crazy," hissed Iris. "I'm a green witch. And I'm telling you, you're about to cut down a perfectly healthy hundred-and-fifty-year-old elm tree."

At the mention of Iris being a witch, the workers froze. The bearded man and his heavyset partner glanced at each other nervously.

"It's not our call," the heavyset one said, holding his hands up like Iris was pointing a gun at him. "When the lanternflies find a tree like this, it becomes kinda like their homebase. They breed and spread and then all of a sudden there's ten times as many of them. We *hafta* cut this tree down, lady. I'm sorry."

Iris spread her arms wider and the two workers in front

jumped. One in the back, who was older than the others and had wrinkled, leathery skin, threw his head back and said, "Enough of this shit. I can't wait until Keller gets elected."

He marched forward, pushing the younger, larger men out of the way and picked up the chainsaw, wielding it like a sword pointed at Iris. He pulled its cord and the blade whirred to life.

"Get out of the way, witch," he said over the roar of the chainsaw.

Iris braced herself. Would this man really attack her? Her heart was racing so fast she couldn't think straight, her eyes darting around the park lawn, looking for any plants she might be able to call upon for help. There was only grass and a few weedy flowers, nothing that would do more than maybe slow the leathery-skinned worker's steps for a half-second.

The worker took a step forward with the chainsaw still pointed at Iris.

"Please," begged Iris. "Don't do this."

"You wanna be a treehugger?" asked the worker. "Go find your own fucking city to do it in." He took another step forward.

Just then, Delilah came racing over the hill as fast as she could in her pencil skirt, holding both her pumps and Iris's heels in her hands. She looked from Iris to the workers, and when she spotted the whirring chainsaw, she rushed to Iris's side.

"Hey, hey, hey, let's just calm down now," she said.

The arrival of a death witch rattled the workers even more and made the older worker finally pause his slow approach. He looked back, realizing it was just him in front of the two witches, an annoyed and anxious expression on his face that his buddies had left him all alone. He lowered the chainsaw.

"Tree's coming down," he announced. "Move or we'll get the park precinct to move you."

Keeping her eyes on the park workers, Delilah said to Iris: "What's going on? What are you guys arguing about?"

"They're going to cut down the tree," said Iris. "But it's healthy, like, totally healthy. It just has those bugs on it."

"Lanternflies," said the older worker. "Pests. Like you two are being. Move!"

Delilah looked at the elm tree and seemed to get lost in her thoughts for a moment. She set both pairs of shoes down and turned back to the workers.

"So, all you need are these bugs gone?" she asked them.

"We'll spray 'em once the tree's down," the older worker said.

Then Iris watched Delilah do something she'd never seen before. The pale woman, still in her vintage 90s suit and contoured makeup, held up her hands to the tree and closed her eyes. For a moment nothing happened. Then, one by one, the lanternflies began to fall to the ground. It was a trickle at first, then several at a time, and then *dozens*, until it looked like the tree had shed an entire bloom of lanternfly-like leaves onto the grass, the dead insects even landing on Delilah's shoulders and on top of her fauxhawk. But she kept her focus until every last lanternfly was on the ground.

"What the fuck..." said the older worker, his voice quavering.

Delilah wasn't finished. Once the tree was stripped of its pests, Delilah kneeled down and put her hands to the ground. She took a deep breath in and Iris could see her hands shaking as the bodies of the lanternflies decomposed at super speed, leaving behind a thin bed of dark, decayed insect matter. When she stood back up, she could barely keep her balance, needing to grab the tree trunk for support. Iris saw there was a sheen of sweat on Delilah's face and she looked even more pale than usual.

"Are you okay?" whispered Iris.

"I think I'm gonna throw up," said Delilah as she leaned her head against the tree.

People had begun to gather around the tree, several of them with their phones out to record the confrontation. Two police officers were also making their way towards the scene and Iris saw the heavyset worker go off to greet them. All around them rose excited, nervous chatter:

"Did she just kill all those bugs?" "That's a death witch, isn't it?" "Holy shit that was wild." "Now imagine she decides to do that on a crowded subway." "Yooo I can't wait to see the memes." "They and all the rest of the freaks should have to go live in their own country or something. They can't be here with us."

"Delilah... I think we should get out of here," said Iris.

Delilah nodded and Iris grabbed their shoes. As the two of them walked away from the tree, they were stopped by the police officers and the heavyset park worker.

"Ma'am, why don't you come on down to the station so we can

have a chat about your, uh, disagreement with Park Services?" one of the cops said to Iris, keeping an eye fixed on Delilah.

"No thank you," said Delilah in a strained voice.

The other cop stepped forward. "We really think–"

Delilah held up her hand. It was trembling.

"We're going home now," she said. "And if I come back tomorrow and see this tree is gone, I'm going to take you up on your offer to go to the precinct after all." Keeping her hand held out, Delilah took a shaky step forward and said: "Have a nice day, officers."

The officers stared at Delilah's hand for several agonizing moments, the spectators around them gasping and stepping away from the witches. Finally, the officers moved to the side to let Delilah and Iris pass. No one else stopped them as Iris hurried them to the street as fast as Delilah's pace would allow, flagging down the first taxi she saw.

Do It For The Likes

~IRIS~

It was Iris's turn to play nurse, though there wasn't much she could do after Delilah ran to the bathroom as soon as they got home. She stayed there for the next three hours getting sick into the toilet until she was dry heaving so loud it was making Iris queasy.

Iris tried her best though, putting two pitchers of water by the bathroom door and then going out to get Delilah a large bottle of Pedialyte. When Delilah emerged at last, Iris saw that she hadn't had a single drop of hydration of any sort, the death witch's color thankfully looking back to its usual pale marble instead of the sickly yellow-bone from earlier.

"Please hydrate a little," Iris begged her. "If you don't want the water or the Pedialyte, I can go out and get you whatever you want."

With shuffling steps, Delilah fetched the massive jug of the grape-flavored, now lukewarm Pedialyte, not bothering to chill it before she unscrewed the top and started drinking. After a long gulp that left purple rivulets running down Delilah's chin, she sat on the living room's hardwood floor, declining Iris's offer to let her have the saggy couch.

"Pretty gross, huh?" asked Delilah.

It took Iris a minute to catch on that Delilah wasn't talking about the Pedialyte but what she'd done at Central Park.

"You saved that tree," said Iris, still awe-struck by how Delilah was willing to act so boldly in public.

"And killed probably a thousand of those bugs. *And* threatened some park workers and a couple cops." She held up a fist and pumped it weakly in the air. "A grand victory for the public image of death witches everywhere."

"The lanternflies were going to die anyway. You heard that old guy, they were going to spray them after they cut down the tree. That spray probably would've killed a bunch of the grass too and who knows what else."

Delilah gulped down another mouthful of the Pedialyte, wiping her mouth with the back of her hand. "Yeah, I'm a regular hero," she said glumly.

"Well, why did you do it then?" Iris asked quietly.

Delilah didn't answer her. She looked down at the now half-empty Pedialyte bottle, making the purple liquid slosh from side to side.

Iris opened her mouth to speak and then shut it again. Delilah had put herself at real risk for that elm tree–and for Iris. She could've just let Iris run off like a lunatic into Central Park or pulled her away from the park workers or given up the second she saw the police were involved, but she stood her ground. And here she was, still in her vintage blazer and too-tight pencil skirt with her nylons torn and such a guilty, wretched look like she'd just single-handedly blotted out the sun and cast the world into darkness.

Iris stared at Delilah until the woman realized Iris was trying to get her attention.

"I didn't like what you said earlier," Iris said.

"To the police?" asked an exhausted Delilah.

"No, about your face," said Iris.

Delilah furrowed her brow, clearly having no clue what Iris was talking about.

"You said people were going to see your face and have you burned at the stake."

"Oh, *that*. I was just being dramatic," said Delilah.

"I didn't like it," Iris said again. She kept her hazel eyes trained on Delilah's pale blue ones, refusing to break first.

"Relax, they don't burn witches anymore," Delilah said.

"That's not what I mean, and you know it. I like your face. I think… I think it's beautiful," said Iris. As soon as the words were out, Iris's courage abandoned her and she looked away, sure that at any moment Delilah was going to start cutting her down to size with biting sarcasm.

Delilah put the Pedialyte bottle down and shrugged off her

blazer, the sleeveless black blouse underneath accentuating her chest and strong shoulders. Iris was surprised to see a tattoo on Delilah's left shoulder of two ravens flying away from each other. It was the only tattoo Iris had ever seen on Delilah and it looked like it had more than a few years on it.

"As long as we're saying things we don't like hearing…" started Delilah.

Oh boy, here we go, thought Iris.

"Stop saying you're going to run off into the woods." Delilah lifted her head and gave Iris a weak grin. "I really don't want to have to find another roommate."

Iris's throat was very dry. "It's a deal then," she said, getting up off the loveseat and walking over to Delilah. "You stop saying you have an ugly face and I'll stop saying I'm going to run away to the woods." She held out her hand so they could shake on it.

Delilah reached up and wrapped her hand around Iris's. Just like the other night, it was cool to the touch.

"Deal," said Delilah. She pressed her thumb softly into the back of Iris's hand and then let go. Then she added: "Does that offer to go out and get me something still stand?"

"Of course," said Iris, beaming.

Delilah held her stomach. "Great, 'cause I'm starving. Can you get us some pizza?"

"Your wish is my desire," teased Iris.

~DELILAH~

Delilah spent the next few days expecting the worst, convinced that the parks department or the police or some random asshole on social media would track her down after the scene at Central Park. And even though no one came, she was extra careful to keep her hood up when she was in public and even started to powder her face and hands to make her look a little more "normal".

She also took what Iris had said to heart, even if she wasn't ready to believe it. Throughout the day, she looked at herself on her phone, trying to find a pose that made Delilah actually like what she saw. She tried out camera modes and filters, taking dozens of snaps and not liking a single one of them. But she stayed true to her word, holding back her snarky comments when Iris was around and trying her hardest not to let how much she hated the way she looked slip out.

Frankly, her looks weren't top of mind anyway, for a change. Delilah was much more occupied thinking about how Iris had thrown herself in front of a goddamn chainsaw to protect a tree. A tree! That and their impending eviction and doomed lawsuit, of course. But what really transfixed Delilah was seeing just how much her green witch roommate was willing to put on the line for what she gave a shit about. Would Delilah do the same? *Could* Delilah do the same? She had no fucking clue.

Delilah wracked her brain for any way to get their neighbors to take a shine to her and Iris, making a point to walk through parks small and large looking for trees that had been taped off and marked for cutting. She didn't know two shits about trees, but she was able to recognize the spotted lanternflies easily enough, and every time she saw a tree–taped off or not–with the flitting little pests all over it, Delilah nonchalantly walked over, put her hands up to the tree, and killed every last one of them, walking away before anyone got nosey about what she was up to.

She didn't enjoy seeing the insect carcasses dropping to the ground in droves, though it was unsettling how the more she did it, the easier it became. One of the advantages of being a death witch, she guessed. Even so, she took the extra time–and the extra nausea that came with it–to decompose the lanternflies, making a bed of fresh mulch for new things to grow.

I might be a piece of shit but just like shit, I can help make room for something better, she thought.

Delilah tried asking people over text if they had any ideas to either soothe their neighbors or stop the building's sale, but everyone she messaged only had ho-hum condolences and unrealistic, absurd suggestions that were sure to get her and Iris in even hotter water than they were now. One thought kept nagging at the back of Delilah's mind–she was, whether she liked it or not, a death witch. If she really put her mind to it, she could probably score a job making mid six figures in a few weeks, more than enough to pay down any bullshit lawsuits and find her *and* Iris–together or separately–new places to live.

But there would be no coming back from that. Once a money-grubbing death witch, always a money-grubbing death witch. She couldn't do that, not yet, no matter how much she wanted to spare Iris the fuckery they were going through.

When Delilah got home after exterminating the lanternflies from six different trees, Iris greeted her with puppy dog excitement.

"They wrote back!" she exclaimed.

"Who?" Delilah asked, slightly concerned that her nausea attacks were beginning to totally fade after a few days of killing things. What other effects might regular use of her death magick have?

"Andrea and Jacob. Arthur's kids. I wrote to them–without mentioning that note we got, obviously–and asked them why they were selling after their dad had done such a great job with this place for so long."

"We've only been here a year…" Delilah said.

"They don't know that," said Iris.

"And did he *really* do a great job with it?" asked Delilah. "The tile in the hallway is cracked, the lot out across from the building is practically a garbage dump with all the old furniture and weeds, and the basement storage has been locked since we moved in."

Seeing the annoyed look on Iris's face, Delilah backed off.

"Okay, whatever. What did they say?" she asked.

"I didn't read the email yet. I was waiting for you," said Iris.

Delilah rolled her eyes with a groan, trying not to show her smile over Iris's sweet little gesture. "Well open it–I can already feel my disappointment. Maybe we'll be really lucky and they'll decide they want to sue us too," she said.

Iris opened the email, her eyes scanning the response. Her pensive expression melted into frowning sadness.

"Oh god," said Delilah. "That bad?"

Tears welled in Iris's eyes, a heavy drop rolling down her honey-brown cheek.

"Iris…?" Delilah wondered what the green witch could be so upset about. She made an instinctive move to go over and comfort Iris but held herself back.

"They thanked me for my note," said a sniffling Iris. "And for what I said about Arthur. They told me that since he died so suddenly, they can't bear the thought of being here because it reminds them of him…" Iris wiped the tear away, her body heaving with a low, soft cry.

"Oh" was Delilah's only reply, having expected something much worse. She reached a hand towards Iris and then stopped. Naturally, death didn't make Delilah feel uncomfortable–but people's reaction to it did; all the crying and grieving was alien to Delilah, who couldn't remember a single death in her adult life that was more to her than a cloudy day. She drummed her fingers on her thighs as tried not to watch Iri cry.

"So… I guess that's that then," said Delilah. "At least we tried. It was a good idea."

Iris continued to softly sob as she stared at her phone and Delilah remembered then what Iris had said about her own parents being gone. She tried to change the subject.

"I didn't come up with any great ideas today, but I did find a bunch more trees with those lanternflies all over them," said Delilah. "They're mulch now. Have you looked up anything about these things? People *hate* them. Probably more than they hate paras. There's a bunch of articles pretty much begging people to go and stomp them out, and even as a death witch I think that's wild. Too bad our neighbors can't see us killing those bugs, we might actually score some sympathy points."

Iris looked up from her phone. "Maybe we can," she said.

Delilah could see the gears turning in Iris's head. "How? Are we gonna make our own indie film all about killing spotted lanternflies or something? Sounds riveting."

"No, not a film–we can put it on social media," said Iris. "TikTok, YouTube, all that stuff."

Like everyone else her age, Delilah binged social media but she sure didn't know how to make any of the stuff she watched. Did Iris? She was beginning to feel awful at how she'd judged the green witch the past year, assuming she was just some hippie flower girl.

"I can take care of the bugs if you can take care of the social media," said Delilah.

Iris smiled warmly. "Leave it to me," she said.

They didn't have trouble finding two more trees covered in lanternflies, one in the East River Park and another near the Bowery. Iris made Delilah pose in a handful of positions before she took care of the pests for real, Iris walking excitedly around Delilah as she tried to capture Delilah's death magick like she was filming a Hollywood blockbuster. A few people stared curiously on as Delilah cleared the trees, but thankfully no one was interested in getting any closer than that. Once Delilah had composted the bugs, Iris did her part, sprinkling seeds into the fresh dirt and cooing to them to sprout. Afterwards they popped back into Anyway Bar. It was earlier and quieter than the last time, with only two other customers besides Iris and Delilah.

Delilah explained their plan to Ruth.

"It could work," said Ruth with begrudging confidence. "I think Coven Hub offers some guides for this kind of thing if you want." She was in a hoodie with the sleeves cut off and a loose pair of jeans, having just buzzed and dyed her hair blonde a day or two ago. Iris had been right without realizing it–Delilah *had* hooked up with Ruth, though it felt like a million years ago now and it had been just a one-time thing, like so many of Delilah's flings and hookups.

"I already made us accounts," said Iris, fully absorbed in her phone. "All with the same usernames and everything."

"Now we just have to get famous," said Delilah, still wondering how anyone got people to view their posts.

"I'll send your stuff around," said Ruth, peeking over the bar at Iris's screen. "I've got a bunch of people who follow me for my tat work. And hey, think about it this way–even if this fails miserably, at least you guys saved some trees, ya?"

"Thanks for the vote of confidence," said Delilah in a droll tone.

"Delilah saved those trees," Iris added. "I just watched."

Delilah's heart skipped a beat at the timbre of Iris's voice that sounded not just defensive of Delilah's effort but proud of her too.

"Let's just call it a team effort," said Ruth, setting down three small shot glasses in front of them. She took a bottle from the bar's top shelf–Weller 12, a pricey favorite of Delilah's she could rarely afford–and poured out shots, keeping Iris's smaller than the other two.

"To witchcraft," said Ruth, holding up her shot.

The three of them clinked their glasses and drank their bourbon, Delilah and Ruth setting their glasses upside down on the bartop, which was covered in Ruth's doodlings during slow shifts. When the glasses hit the wood, a stampede of exaggerated animals took off running to the other end of the bar, tumbling and reforming into a stylized skyline of New York shaped from the stacked shapes of the stampeding animals.

"That's... smooth," said Iris, sipping her small shot.

"It better be," said Delilah. "It's like forty a shot."

Iris's eyes went wide.

Delilah inched her glass towards Ruth suggestively. "It'd be a shame if a little extra spilled in there," she said, flipping the shot glass back over.

Ruth scoffed. She poured Delilah and herself another shot. "This one's for the trees, not for you," she said to Delilah. "At the rate you're going you're gonna wind up a green witch yourself."

"Sign me up," said Delilah, the whiskey hitting her. "So far I'm liking green witches a hell of a lot more than death witches."

If Iris heard Delilah, she didn't show it and Delilah was grateful, feeling silly for what she said. Iris was busy squinting at her phone in frustration. "I'm sorry, I think I need to be home to do this. Do you mind?" she asked Delilah.

"Hey if you don't like my bar, you can just say so," joked Ruth, eyeing Delilah for her reaction.

"No, it's great–especially when it's quiet," Iris said, setting her half-finished shot on the bar. "I just, uh... I'm having trouble focusing."

"I bet," muttered Ruth under her breath so that only Delilah could hear her. Delilah shot her a dirty look.

"Yeah go ahead, I'll meet you back home," said Delilah.

Iris gave her and Ruth a cheery wave and padded out of the bar, Delilah watching as she left, enjoying how her billowy white harem pants showed off the green witch's delectable ass. She idly wondered if Iris knew the neon pink panties she had on could be seen through her pants, torn between wanting to tell her and not wanting to deprive herself of the eye candy.

"She got them 'looksies' on for you, ya?" asked Ruth, pouring the rest of Iris's shot into Delilah's glass.

"Looksies? What the hell is that?"

"You know, 'come get a looksie at these panties I have on,'" said Ruth, smirking. "Bet she wants you to get an even closer look. I saw you two going at it the other night."

"That was... stupid," said Delilah. "You know me, I'm the master of stupid."

"Didn't look stupid to me. Looked like you were having *fun*.

Flower girl too."

Delilah knocked twice on the bartop. "Don't call her that, she doesn't like it," she said.

"You *do* like her," said Ruth. She nodded approvingly. "I'm not surprised. She's hot, in that lipstick and high heels way. I personally like a few more piercings. But you knew that already."

"Ruthie," Delilah warned.

"Del," Ruth shot back.

Delilah laughed and shook her head. She wasn't about to get into a debate with Ruth about girls.

"I don't wanna freak out Iris, but I'm getting worried about this whole lawsuit thing. The Basilisk was no help and I can *feel* that the climate in the building's changed. It's never been friendly, but I don't run into any neighbors anymore, like everyone's watching through their peepholes to make sure I'm not around before they leave their apartments."

"Sure you're not just being paranoid?" Ruth asked.

"I tried it out when Iris was at work yesterday," said Delilah. "I listened by the door to hear for people coming down the stairs and when I heard footsteps, I opened my door. Whoever it was froze and waited until I closed my door again to keep going down the stairs."

"You know if you guys need a place to crash for a bit, my place isn't huge, but you can stay. The three of us can share a bed." Ruth grinned.

"In your dreams," mumbled Delilah.

"Yours too, my sweet and sour Delilah," said Ruth, putting away the bottle of Weller. As she stood on her tippy toes to return the bottle, the back of her hoodie rose up to reveal a tattoo of a large, napping Chinese lion across Ruth's taut, lean lower back, just above the string hem of the bartender's black thong. The lion opened its eyes as Delilah looked at it and gave her a lazy wink.

"You need to get laid," said Ruth as she slotted the bottle on the backbar, laughing as the tattooed Chinese lion rolled over on its side and then dived down to where Delilah couldn't see.

No Invitation Needed

~IRIS~

Iris wasn't one for deception and was unsurprisingly pretty awful at it. The few times she did manage to get a lie over on someone, she usually confessed before long, unable to handle knowing there was a burning secret between her and someone else. Other people though, they seemed so comfortable with lying that Iris figured her bumbling honesty was just another one of those green witch things, another proof point that she just didn't understand what made people tick.

But she thought–hoped–that neither Delilah nor Ruth suspected she had left not because she needed time alone at home to work on their social media posts but for another reason.

Iris walked into Delilah's room with five paper cup planters grasped in each hand, every one of them with a cut leaf and stem from her creeper vines. She set them along Delilah's walls, spacing them as best she could, and then positioned herself in the center of the room. This was going to hurt, she knew. Most of her green magick left Iris feeling a little tired and maybe crampy, but she was about to attempt something she'd never done before. If she succeeded, it would be the biggest feat of magick she'd ever done.

Iris closed her eyes. In the dark of her vision, she could see the ten paper cup planters like little blue flames spread out around her, aligned along the grid of the walls of Delilah's room.

Grow, she thought. Then louder and more pleadingly she pushed the idea out: *Grow!*

The little blue flames extended upwards, going from candlelight to flaming torch to a jetting inferno, the fiery neon blue reaching all the way up to where the ceiling was and then, remarkably, across it in a spiderweb pattern.

Keep growing, Iris thought. *Let's cover everything.* She was starting to feel fatigued.

The blue flame spider web filled in its empty spaces, turning the dark patches neon blue until the darkness behind Iris's eyes was enveloped by four walls and a ceiling of piercing brilliant blue. She felt an aching pain in her lower back, like someone had punched her in the kidney. It was jarring but not the end of the world–she could go on. Sucking in a breath, she continued.

And flower, she thought out into the dark void of her vision.

Along the neon blue expanse, tiny pockets of sparkling lavender erupted. There was no rhyme or reason to where they took root, but after one shining blossom, two more followed, then four, and then eight after that. Soon there was a constellation of the lavender blooms against the blue and Iris knew if she did any more, she'd barely be able to stand.

She opened her eyes.

The inside of Delilah's room was carpeted in dark green creeping vines and blush pink flowers yawning from their leaves. Already Iris could smell their faint pollen aroma. The scent was sweet and lush and it helped to keep Iris from fainting where she stood.

It took immense concentration for Iris to undress. Her fingers fumbled with the clasps of her top and the elastic waistband of her pants, but she slowly stripped down to just pink lace panties and nothing else, kicking her clothing to one corner of Delilah's room. Adrenaline coursed through her and a war waged in her head between thinking this was going to backfire spectacularly and how she was absolutely *swooning* for Delilah after what she'd done to help those infested trees. It was an infatuation unlike any she'd ever known, the idea that another witch–or anyone, for that matter–could care as much about nature as she did made her bubble with excitement. She laid down on the mattress on the floor. It was as uncomfortable as she'd thought it would be, but she took the opportunity to regain her strength and browse the books on Delilah's table, careful to hold them by the covers as much as she could so she wouldn't have to feel the dead trees on the pages.

There were notes inside–sometimes in the margins, sometimes above an underlined passage, though Iris couldn't make heads or tails of the scribble. Simple, cryptic phrases like "obviously" or "you could've fooled me" peppered the pages, leaving Iris to wonder how many of them belonged to Delilah and how many had been left by other readers. As Iris looked through Delilah's books, the vines continued to thicken and yield more and more vibrant pink flowers; soon the air was thick with their scent.

She heard the apartment door unlock and open. Iris put the book she was reading back and waited, shifting her body into the most seductive pose she could imagine, her arms up over her head and one leg over the other so that her lace panties were pressed outward like its own jungle flower. She held her breath.

Delilah clomped into her room and froze mid-step.

Iris had been going over lines in her head for an hour and even though she felt hot with embarrassment, she said: "Okay, you've seen my underwear. Now I want to see yours." She heard her voice crack with anxiety.

Delilah didn't seem to know what to do. She looked back into the living room and then at Iris, gesturing wordlessly with her hands, not knowing if she should look away or sneak glances at the green witch. Once she'd gotten over her shock, she threw her hand over her face, pale eyes visible through her fingers.

"What're you doing?!" asked Delilah.

The words were a needle that popped Iris's ballooning excitement and she had to fight the urge to hide herself under the bed sheet. Her swooning desire for Delilah felt tiny compared to the racing thoughts about how utterly stupid she must look. Did she really just get half-naked and lounge on her roommate's bed like she was in some cheesy movie? Oh god, she was even worse at dealing with people than she thought…

Then Delilah noticed the thick vines along the walls of her room, her gaze tracing their pathway up to admire the large, blooming pink flowers that swayed and fluttered in the phantom breeze of Iris's green magick. The pale witch's mouth fell open and she reached up to stroke the petals of one of the delicate flowers.

"You did this just now, while I was out…" she said, letting out a giddy laugh as the vine leaves inched up to stroke Delilah's hand in kind. "This is incredible." Delilah's line of sight fell back to Iris; the green witch could feel she was doing her best to keep her eyes on Iris's face and nowhere else. "But why...?"

Okay, thought Iris. *Now's your moment. Don't chicken out–just say what you feel.*

"You saved those trees and you even went out of your way to do so. You… we… green witches are loners, probably more than any other kind of witch. I always thought that, like, I'd always work my magick alone, that no one else would see or care what I did. But working with you today, with my magick and yours and…" Iris took a shaky breath. "I just wanted to thank you for being you, Delilah."

Delilah shifted her weight back and forth and chewed her lower lip. Iris had never seen her like this–she looked positively nervous, a touch of warm blush rising in her ashen cheeks.

"You didn't have to take your clothes off to thank me," she said after a long, weighty pause. Her faint eyebrows turned upwards and a guilty look came over her.

"The vines and flowers are my way of saying thank you," Iris said softly. "Me taking my clothes off is my way of saying… I want you."

Iris swallowed hard as she waited to see what Delilah would say to that. The room was silent and the concentrated smell of wildflowers made it feel tropical and humid, a blessing for Iris as she felt the teeth-chattering chill of anxiety take root in her stomach.

"I… I don't know if I can," said Delilah, her voice so quiet it was nearly a whisper.

"You don't have to do anything," said Iris. "Just lie here with me."

Delilah took a small step forward and Iris stopped her.

"Lie here like I am," Iris said, motioning to her almost nude form.

The blush in Delilah's cheeks got darker. "Okay, but I can't get undressed if I'm being watched…"

With the playful rush of anticipation, Iris flipped over onto her stomach. She felt the warmth of the bed against her cold, goosebumped skin. Then she reached down to pull off her panties, her motions slow and languid to give Delilah as much a show as the death witch wanted, leaving Iris completely naked on the bed. In the quiet of the room, Iris heard zippers being undone and the shuffling sound of Delilah shimmying out of her hip-hugging jeans. She felt the weight of Delilah coming onto the mattress before she felt the woman's cool hand on her back; Iris turned to the side and the two of them were face to face, Delilah having closed the door so that there was only a trickle of light coming in from under the door.

Iris desperately wanted to look at Delilah's naked body but resisted, not wanting to overdo it. Instead, she wrapped an arm around Delilah's back and inched them closer so that their nipples brushed against one another and their legs intertwined, Iris able to feel the light scratch of Delilah on her thigh; her skin might've been cool but down there she was as warm as any other woman, witch or not.

"I'm sorry about the other night," said Delilah. Her light eyes seemed to glow in the dark. "You didn't do anything wrong. I just have some weird hang-ups…"

"Me too. That I'm sorry, I mean. Though I have hang-ups too," said Iris, feeling Delilah's long-fingered hand rest on the swell of her hip. That hand traced its way along Iris's side, one thumb brushing her breast, and then cradled Iris's head before Delilah gently held the fake tresses of Iris's wig.

"I'm taking this off now," said Delilah.

It wasn't a question. Despite Iris's nerves, she luxuriated in the feeling of Delilah taking control and carefully, Delilah pulled the wig away. With a dramatic flair tossed it off the bed, grinning at Iris in the dark.

"Much better," said Delilah. She went to stroke Iris's scalp and Iris snatched her hand.

"Hangups, remember?" Iris moved Delilah's hand down to her chest and placed her cool palm on one breast, pressing so the pale witch could feel her heartbeat. Iris took a deep breath, and mixed in with the scent of jungly wildflowers she could smell something else.

"What is that?" she asked, sniffing at Delilah's neck.

"Or just this, uh, perfume I like. It's got patchouli and some other things," Delilah said, her voice tense.

"No, not that," said Iris. "Whatever it's covering up."

She trailed her button nose down Delilah's neck, feeling a bit silly as she tried to sniff out the scent. She nuzzled herself against the crook of Delilah's armpit.

"Don't!" said Delilah, pulling away.

"But I like it," said Iris. "It's like… motor oil or wet leather. I don't know, it somehow reminds me of New York."

"Yeah, nothing smells sexier than New York City," said Delilah uneasily.

Iris took another sniff. "But I also smell smoke–and it's not coming from you."

Delilah joined in on the sniffing and then bolted upright in bed. "I smell smoke too."

As she got up off the mattress, Iris caught a glimpse of her statuesque, almost ghostly form before Delilah pulled on her jeans and threw on her leather jacket. She rushed out of the room, Iris wrapping the bedsheet like a toga around her and rushing out after.

~DELILAH~

Delilah could see smoke billowing in from under the apartment door, the plume dark and acrid-smelling. Something was burning in the hallway.

"Shit shit shit," she said, pulling open the apartment door before she could even think to check how hot the knob was.

Right in front of their door was a cheap polyester pointy witch hat that someone had set on fire. The flames were small but growing fast, not giving Delilah enough time to put on her boots to stomp it out; instead she picked up one of her Doc Martens and attacked the witch hat like it was a giant water bug trying to scurry into their apartment. Loud smashing echoed through the building's hallway but Delilah didn't care, happy to let the whole damn building hear what was going on.

"Oh my god!" cried Iris as she saw the still-smoking witch hat. She had to take little shuffling steps with Delilah's bed sheet wrapped tightly around her and, even as Delilah smothered the fire, she couldn't help but feel jealous of that sheet.

"I got it out," said Delilah, huffing and puffing. She propped the apartment door open with her boot to air the smoke out. "But I can't believe this. What asshole would light a fire in an apartment building?"

Her question was answered when a wiry man in a ski mask and an old camouflage outfit came darting around the corner, his phone pointed out like a pistol. Its camera light blinded

Delilah and Iris.

"And *this* is their Satanic den," he said dramatically, the stink of alcohol on his breath. "This is where they practice their dark witchcraft and probably drink the blood of innocents to fuel their alliance with Satan!"

"Witches pray to Abaddon, not Satan you jackass," said Delilah, holding a hand up to block out the camera light.

"Delilah, don't," said Iris.

"Delilah! Betrayer of Samson!" the man cried out, shoving his phone in Delilah's face. Being so close, Delilah could tell the man was indeed very, very drunk. "Try to harm me and the world will see!"

Harming that moron was exactly what Delilah wanted to do but she could see Iris pleading with her from behind the man, shaking her head. Following Delilah's line of sight, the masked man turned the phone on Iris.

"And what the hell is this?" He pushed the phone towards Iris's petaled scalp with a grimace. "Like it's said in Revelations: I saw a beast coming out of the sea. It had ten horns and seven heads, with ten crowns on its horns, and on each head a blasphemous name."

Seeing Iris's self-consciousness flare up under the drunken, rabid sermonizing, Delilah shouldered her way between Iris and the masked man. "That's enough, you're done. Go home and sober up," she said, barely able to hold her temper any longer.

"Or what, witch? Gonna drain the life force from me? I saw you threaten those men!"

Ah, shit. The scene in Central Park, thought Delilah. *There must be footage of me with those cops going around... great, just great.*

"No one's being threatened, okay? But you need to leave. We do not give you permission to be in our apartment," said Delilah.

But the man refused to budge, daring the witches to try to move him by force.

"We aren't bad people," said Iris.

The man scoffed. "You're a plague. You've ruined this city."

There was a steadying flash of anger on Iris's face. "So you like scripture? How about this: Let the land produce vegetation: seed-bearing plants and trees on the land that bear fruit with seed in it. And it was so. And God saw that it was good."

Did she just quote the bible? thought an incredulous Delilah.

Iris then closed her eyes tightly as the dark, ropey vines from Delilah's room wound their way past her doorframe and into the living room. The masked man looked up, stunned, lowering his phone to his side.

Out from the snaking vine tendrils emerged a single, large pink-and-white bud that grew at a rapid clip until it had long, silken petals. The petals slowly opened up to reveal a sunny center. The masked man stared at it, awe-struck, and Delilah caught herself staring at it too, amazed at how Iris could make something so beautiful from nothing.

Iris opened her eyes. For a second it looked like she might faint. She said to the man: "Now tell me, does that look 'blasphemous' to you? No, it's…" She looked at the flower like she was being reunited with an old friend. "…it's beautiful. I know there are people out there saying you should be scared of witches and all the other paras, but you know what? We're people, just like you. And lots of us love this city too and want it to be beautiful–for everyone."

The vines peeled away from the ceiling, carrying their large, pink-and-white flower with them so that it was offered out to the intruder. He raised his palm and the flower fell into it, little flecks of pollen bouncing into the air. Delilah stared in wonder at the green witch.

For a moment, the surprise flower seemed enough to calm the intruder. He held it close to his face and peered at it, inhaling its aromas with a nostalgic smile on his face. But then his expression hardened again and turned back to Delilah.

"Flowers are one thing," he said, setting the pink-and-white blossom down on the open half-kitchen's countertop with surprising care. "But you… you don't make pretty flowers."

No, I don't, thought Delilah grimly.

Iris jumped to Delilah's defense.

"Hey! She's spent the last few days saving trees infested with lanternflies," she said. Still in her bedsheet toga, she shuffled to get her phone from the coffee table to show the man in the old camo the videos she'd taken of Delilah. "See? She's trying to help.

"So she does kill things," the man said pedantically.

"Only those pests! Like everyone's been doing. You kill mosquitos, right? And I bet you aren't doing it to save trees.

Do you really think she'd be living in this crummy apartment if she were one of those death witches working for some big corporation? She's not like the others. I know it."

Delilah's heart ached. The masked man paused and took in his surroundings, as if seeing the apartment fully for the first time. Not much of his face could be seen under the ski mask, but there was doubt in his eyes.

"You don't have to like us," continued Iris. "That's fine. But you can see for yourself we're not any better off than you probably are. We'll all be on the street in a few weeks and it's going to be a lot harder for us to find a new place to live than for you, I bet…"

Shaking his head fitfully, the intruder said: "You shouldn't have moved in here. Everything was fine before."

"We won't be here for much longer. Even if… even if they decide not to sell the building for some reason, we'll leave. I promise," said Iris.

Iris, what are you doing? thought Delilah. *We don't need to make promises to this asshole.*

But even as Delilah bristled at the thought of having to move out should they somehow keep this building from being torn down, she could see that Iris's pledge was what the masked man needed to hear to feel like he'd done his job. He looked at the large pink-and-white blossom as if he might take it and then inched his way to the apartment door, staying turned towards Delilah and Iris the entire time. He looked from one witch to the other and shook his head in a gesture of disbelief and indignance.

"You shouldn't have moved in here," he said again before he disappeared down the hallway.

Two Broke Witches

~DELILAH~

With the intruder gone, Delilah took the burnt witch hat and threw it in a plastic bag to toss out later. She locked and deadbolted their front door and then marched up to Iris, grabbing the green witch's face in her hands and kissing her. Startled, Iris let go of the bedsheet and the makeshift toga fell to the floor. Delilah sloughed off her leather jacket, nudging Iris back into her room and onto the mattress, the living room lights casting a bright beam into the vine-covered den. Between Iris's legs, Delilah could see faint wisps of pink hair against her umber skin.

"You said you wanted me," said Delilah, undoing the fly of her jeans. "I want you too."

There was a lump in her throat at the thought of Iris seeing her naked and so she didn't stay standing long, kneeling at the edge of the mattress to duck her head between Iris's smooth, warm legs. She started kissing from the ankle up, looking over the jut of the green witch's bare breasts to make sure she wasn't going too fast. Iris gave her a gentle nod–which was a relief because Delilah didn't know if she *could* stop now. It had been one thing to lie naked with Iris and for them to hold each other, but hearing her defend Delilah and seeing how she defused what could've been a much, much worse situation… it sparked a frenzy in Delilah, one of lust and admiration and utter reverence for the green witch that could only be sated with the taste of Iris on Delilah's lips.

Delilah continued to kiss her way up Iris's legs, gripping the green witch's hips in her strong hands. She squeezed her fingers into those hips and walked her fingertips back so that Delilah was grabbing onto Iris's ass, pushing the warm, wet V of the green witch towards her mouth. God, how Delilah wanted her! But she held back, slowing her kissing and teasing Iris by blowing gently on her skin. Iris let out a shuddering sigh and spread her legs wider, rolling herself towards Delilah's mouth, but the death witch kept things slow, enjoying the writhing excitement and growing moans from the woman under her.

She brought the hot stream of blowing air up Iris's thigh and then across the witch's wet lips, admiring the patch of pink hair above. It wasn't like Iris's petaled hair, looking no different than Delilah's, and as Delilah brought her face close to Iris's sex, the fine pink hairs tickled her nose. Delilah breathed in the dizzying, lush scent of the green witch, not knowing if it was that smell that made her heart thump so hard in her chest or if it was because it had been so long since she'd been so close to someone else.

Delilah traced her tongue up along Iris's lips, slowly and strongly, the tip of her tongue making Iris squirm in pleasure.

"Oh god, oh my god," Iris said, clawing at the bedsheets.

Her breathy voice spurred Delilah on and she started to draw her tongue across Iris in a flitting, zigzag motion, licking a lazy Z up and down Iris's lips until she was grinding into Delilah's pale face. She threaded her fingers through Delilah's dark hair to hold her in place and pressed her warm thighs against the death witch's head, cupping her pierced ears. Soon Delilah's face was slick with Iris, the green witch tasting even better than she smelled.

The moment felt unreal. Iris was enjoying this–really enjoying it–and her hands and thighs grabbed Delilah like she couldn't get enough. It made Delilah forget about all those times she'd looked at herself on her phone or in the mirror, disgusted with what she saw and wishing she could've been any other way. She dug her fingers deeper into Iris until the witch let out a moan and drove her tongue inside Iris's sweet, exquisite sex, drawing out a delighted and wondrous laugh from Iris.

The green witch continued to writhe beneath Delilah and she thought that maybe she'd been wrong. Maybe she wasn't a piece of shit after all–not if someone like Iris could feel this way about her. Maybe she really could be happy.

~IRIS~

As Delilah licked her with a practiced tongue, Iris's vision went glassy, the room blurring into dark green sea speckled with pink budding flowers. She clutched Delilah's fauxhawk tightly, loving how it felt to press the other taller, stronger, more formidable witch against the warm V between her legs. Once she'd spoiled herself rotten on Delilah's intoxicating attention, Iris playfully tugged on her hair, bringing Delilah just an inch or two up so that her expert tongue could pleasure Iris in another way.

Delilah was good at licking Iris there too, caressing Iris's pearl with her lips and tongue while Iris let go of Delilah's hair and brought her hands to her breasts to tease her nipples. Iris rolled them both between her fingertips as Delilah found a steady, flicking rhythm that made Iris squeeze Delilah's head tighter between her legs, the touch of Delilah's many piercings making her body quiver even harder. Reading Iris's body language, Delilah quickened her dutiful lapping. It was insistent, imperious worship, the sort that said Delilah was going to make Iris come and come hard, and there was nothing Iris could do to stop her.

Not that she wanted to.

Iris looked down at Delilah just as the other witch looked back up at her, their eyes meeting and holding a joy-soaked stare. Even though Iris couldn't see the bottom of Delilah's face, she could tell she was grinning. They kept looking at one another as Delilah pressed the hot spade of her tongue against Iris and rocked her head from side to side, bringing a crashing wave of ecstasy down on the green witch that made her body tighten like a violin string. Her breath caught in her throat and her back arched as a shuddering orgasm rippled through Iris's body.

She said something, maybe–perhaps it was just a blissed-out moan–and slapped her hands down on the mattress, gripping so tight she thought she'd tear the sheets underneath. Delilah did not let up. She drew her tongue back down and nuzzled her nose against Iris instead, giving the green witch adoring licks that carried Iris along the edge of pleasure, towards what she knew would soon be another ecstatic, mind-fuzzing orgasm.

Iris reached a trembling hand down and pulled Delilah's face up, the living room light catching the wet sheen across the death witch's striking features.

"I want to please you too," said Iris.

"This is pleasing me," said Delilah, panting warm breaths that made Iris tingle.

Iris twisted her lips to the side. "You know what I mean," she said. "Will you let me?"

Delilah clambered onto the bed and Iris took her by the shoulders, noticing once again her twin raven tattoo. She guided the tall, pale witch onto her back as Iris knelt between Delilah's legs. Delilah chewed on her lower lip, making that same nervous look as before, and Iris dipped her head to Delilah's chest to kiss the other woman's breasts, her glossy lips quickly finding one deep purple nipple while her hand slipped down to Delilah's crotch. Delilah wasn't lying–she *was* pleased, not to mention so wet that Iris's fingers slipped into her effortlessly.

It took Delilah a few minutes of Iris's delicate attention to relax, but before long Delilah had her knees bent and legs spread to make room for Iris, with her head leaning back against her pillow as she gave a litany of surprisingly soft sighs for her stature. While Iris had her fingers dancing inside of Delilah, she used her thumb to rub slow, pleasing circles that turned the witch's soft sighs into deeper, throaty moans. This close to Delilah, Iris could fully enjoy her scent. It was strong and distinct, that was for sure, but Iris also found it addictive in some way, taking greedy huffs of that oil-and-leather aroma with every breath.

Iris planted kisses up Delilah's chest and neck, winding her way up further still towards the death witch's delicious, dark mouth. Iris, in her pleasure-drenched fervor, teasingly bit Delilah's lip, her roughhousing igniting Delilah's passion all the more. The tall woman put her hand on top of Iris's and pushed her fingers deeper; with her other hand, she grabbed Iris's ass cheek, squeezing it hard and possessively.

With Delilah's hand guiding Iris, it didn't take long for the death witch to climax. She groaned with primal lust right in Iris's ear and held Iris against her as she gushed against both their hands. Then she let her body go slack and threw her head back, her chest rising and falling with a labored attempt to catch her breath.

"Holy shit," said Delilah with a delirious laugh. "Do you have magick in your fingers or something too?"

Iris kept her hand resting against Delilah's crotch to enjoy the warmth and wetness. "If I do, then you have it in your tongue," she said back, kissing Delilah's ear.

They stayed that way for a few more lovely moments and then Iris rolled to the side to lie next to Delilah. She looked at the twin raven tattoo.

"What's it mean?" Iris asked.

"Oh? That? It's nothing," said Delilah.

Iris nudged Delilah with her hip, their sweaty bodies sliding against each other. "Oh, come on! I just made you, like, you know…"

"I just made you 'you know' too," Delilah shot back with a smile.

"You're really not going to tell me?" asked Iris.

Delilah groaned. "Fine, fine. I got it when I was a teenager though so don't laugh."

"I won't," Iris said softly.

"Okay, so… in Norse mythology, Odin had two ravens. I forget their names but they stood for 'thought' and 'memory' and were supposed to be kind of like his eyes and ears, telling him everything that was happening in the world," Delilah explained.

Iris waited for Delilah to continue like an attentive schoolgirl.

"In most cultures, ravens are all about death," said Delilah. "But in Norse mythology, they symbolize wisdom and are protectors and helpers. I guess, growing up and finding out I was a death witch, I just wanted to believe I might still turn out different too…"

Iris stretched her toes towards Delilah's, stroking them gently.

"I think you have," she said.

They were both very quiet then, looking up at the constellation of pink flowers dotting the vines along the ceiling. Her hand still on Delilah, Iris could feel the woman's heartbeat slowing as they relaxed.

After a while, Delilah said: "Everyone should have a place like this to retreat to."

And then Iris got another idea for how they might save themselves–and the building.

"The lot behind the building!" Iris said.

Delilah turned to her, alabaster cheeks still flushed from her orgasm. "What is it? Do you hear something?" She sat up and twisted towards the curtained window, her pendulous breasts hanging in Iris's face; she fought back the urge to kiss them.

"No, no–I mean, the lot behind the building… what if I made it like in here? You know, like a garden or something. Then all the tenants here can have a place where *they* can retreat to."

"Yeah, for a few more weeks, I guess…" cautioned Delilah.

"Okay, maybe, but who knows–maybe whoever takes the building will keep it," said Iris, her excitement growing, fueled by the time she and Delilah had just enjoyed. "And, like, if we do it couldn't we use that in court if we had to? You know, tell people we tried to make things better and increase the property value or whatever?"

For a moment it looked like Delilah was going to push back again, but then she just snorted a laugh and shook her head. "Sure. Why the hell not? You can post all about it on those accounts you made. What was the name again?"

"Two_Broke_Witches," said Iris.

Delilah snorted another laugh. "Two broke witches… that's us alright."

Iris took Delilah's hand in her own and nuzzled against her, drifting to sleep as she imagined all the ways they might transform the forgotten junkyard lot into something gorgeous and alive.

UNSOLICITED ADVICE

~IRIS~

In the morning, the witches went to inspect the old lot. It was terribly overgrown, some of the weeds inside taller than Iris, with patches of gravel and dry dirt littering the inside between pieces of discarded furniture. Its iron wrought fence was threaded through long dead vines and it was as Iris was checking the vines for life that she discovered the small square plaque marking the lot as property of the city–a public green space in fact, one that was open to use but that had been neglected for a long, long time. Whatever they wanted to do to this lot, they'd need permission from the city first.

Iris and Delilah decided to divide and conquer: Iris would take a closer look at the lot to figure out how much work they had to do and what vegetation would grow best on it; Delilah meanwhile would track down any permits or allowances they needed so they wouldn't wind up in a jail cell for something absurd as criminal acts of gardening.

Considering she was a green witch, Iris felt guilty that she'd gotten the easier job. But as she explored more of the overgrown space, she found herself stumbling through the weedy grass and having to avoid hidden caches of splintered furniture and rusted, sharp metal. She changed into a heavy denim jumpsuit for the rest of her expedition and tried not to think about when her last tetanus shot was.

But even with all the trash, Iris couldn't deny how peaceful it felt to be around so much greenery–even if it was the weedy, pushy variety. She couldn't remember the last time she had been in such a thick patch of vegetation all alone and the serenity of it was like a clog in her sinuses and ears had finally, blissfully gone away. Without even having to try, she could see the colorful auras of the plant life, the rainbow spectrum giving her all kinds of hints about how verdant, sun-starved, or young the plants hidden among the weeds were. She could even hear them clearly without the usual need to focus and learn their specific cadences, the rush of myriad plant-speak not cacophonous like it could so often be in a greenhouse or a flower store but harmonious and familiar, as if these ignored plants had gotten used to each other over the forgotten years.

Iris got so lost in the plantsong that she had actually stopped thinking about the night before for the first time all day. Under her jumpsuit, she could still catch Delilah's smell on her body, not ready to shower it off just yet. She sighed happily. When Iris had left the bar and went back home to set up her surprise for Delilah, she didn't know what to expect. But the night they shared–the intimacy of their bodies and their souls–was more than Iris at her most optimistic could have hoped for. Iris closed her eyes and inhaled Delilah's clinging scent again, imagining the death witch's lips and tongue on her.

"You can't be here," an oddly familiar voice said.

Iris's eyes bolted open. A few feet away was a wiry man with tired eyes and graying hair. He stared at her in terror and Iris realized where she knew him from–he was the man in the ski mask and camo who had rushed into their apartment three night before. She took a nervous step back, her own look of terror making the man's expression soften.

"I'm not going to hurt you," he said, holding up his hands.

Seeing the man's splayed, shaking hands made Iris less afraid, her fear replaced by a surge of anger. "You scared the hell out of us last night," she said. "You think I can't be here? You can't barge into someone's apartment. You're lucky we didn't call the cops on you."

The man gave a small, knowing smile. "But you didn't– because you can't, can you? Cops don't like–" He edited whatever he was going to say and instead said: "People like you and your 'friend'. And it's only going to get worse for you people after the election."

Iris was sick of hearing about the election and Roger Keller, the candidate claiming to be for "real" New Yorkers. She glared at the man.

"This is a public park," she said. "I have every right to be here as you do. And if you must know, we're trying to make it nicer."

The wiry man furrowed his brow. "Why?" he asked.

Iris regretted saying anything, not trusting the same man who had tricked his way into her apartment not to undermine Iris and Delilah's efforts to avoid being sued into the ground.

"We just, like, think it could be nicer..." said Iris, inwardly groaning at her poor attempt to lie.

"Sure," said the man with a smirk. "Listen, honey–"

"Iris."

"Listen, *Iris*."

"And what's your name?" Iris asked, tired of being interrogated by a total stranger.

"Heh. Wouldn't have thought you'd be the pushy one. Name's Marco, alright? And I was gonna say–you seem okay. I don't know about that other one, but you... you almost seem like a native New Yorker."

"I *am* a native New Yorker," said an annoyed Iris. "I'm from Crown Heights."

Marco laughed. "Red Hook for me," he said. "It's a small world, huh?"

Iris made a face to show she found it entirely too small at that moment.

"My point," he continued. "Is that it seems like the, uhm, stuff you do isn't so bad. Those plants and that flower... it was actually kinda pleasant, but don't go quoting me on that. But it's a big country. Don't you think you might be happier somewhere else? Somewhere more naturey maybe?"

The tall, willowy weeds around Iris moved away from her as she bristled with anger. "Are you saying I can't live in the city I grew up in?" she asked. For a split second, Iris was about to press Marco about the civil suit but held her tongue at the last moment, worried she'd make things worse.

Marco held his hands up again. "I'm just saying maybe you don't want to be in New York when the other shoe drops."

"And what does *that* mean?" asked Iris.

He gave her a sorry look and then started to back away. "I'm not gonna narc on you for being in this lot, but someone else might. And some cops, they're just looking for any excuse to rough up people like you. Just some food for thought. And one other thing..."

"What?" snapped Iris, feeling like she was channeling Delilah.

"If this really is public park space, you can just call the Department of Sanitation to take all this garbage away. Legally they have to. Trust me, I worked for them for thirty years."

Marco nodded an awkward goodbye to Iris and then walked off the lot, leaving her alone again. As soon as he was out of sight, the soothing plantsong returned, the feeling more calming than any fancy shot of whiskey. Iris sat down on the ground and wondered how she was going to tell Delilah about her encounter with Marco without the death witch flipping out.

~DELILAH~

Looking up permits was a nightmare. Delilah started with a few simple searches and then went down a rabbit hole of shitty government websites and outdated Quora and Reddit posts that led her back to a single hotline number she'd already tried and given up on thanks to its excruciating wait time. She was so desperate that she considered reaching out to Coven Hub for help but didn't know if she could stomach putting up with all the hoops they made witches jump through.

Being on hold at least gave her time to think about Iris. In the light of day, she felt sheepish about the whole thing, sure that she must have come off like some clumsy, out of practice loser compared to the dainty and elegant green witch. Delilah tried to remember how she'd used her hands and mouth. Had she been too grabby? Too desperate? What about when Iris was touching her–had it been pushy to guide Iris like she had, like she was afraid the green witch would move her hand away if she didn't? In the moment she was lust-drunk but looking back, she seemed so... lame.

Iris though, she was perfect. She felt and smelled and tasted *so good*, everything about the green witch brimming with a lush sensuality that made Delilah warm in the cheeks just to think about. Delilah could've spent the entire night kneeling between Iris's legs and kissing every inch of her umber skin, and as she started imagining tracing her lips down Iris's neck and chest, along her waist, her hips, and even the pert curve of her ass, she squirmed, realizing she was getting wet.

The hold music ended and an impatient operator came on the line. Delilah stumbled out of her daydream and through her permit questions; it took several mush-brained attempts, but she finally phrased her request in terms that made sense.

"So… you want to know if you can volunteer to improve a public garden?" the operator asked over the line.

"Yes," said Delilah, trying to recenter herself.

"Have you spoken to GreenThumb yet?"

"No…? Who is that?" asked Delilah.

The operator sighed. "New York City has an organization called GreenThumb that helps support community gardens. Once you've applied with them, they'll provide tools and support to help you with your garden. You can apply at their website and you should hear back in four to six weeks once they've processed your request," explained the operator in a droll voice.

Delilah didn't have four to six weeks. If she and Iris were going to make this garden work, they needed to move fast.

"Is there any way to expedite the application process?" asked Delilah. "We, you know, we just don't want to miss peak gardening season."

She had no idea when "peak gardening season" was, hoping the operator didn't either.

There was another sigh, this one longer and more frustrated.

"You can try visiting their office directly to see if they'll speed things up for you," said the operator.

"Great. Where's that?"

"It's off 5th Avenue and 64th Street, in Central Park. Right next to the zoo."

Delilah's stomach churned. She'd been hoping to avoid Central Park for a while after what happened with the park workers.

"Okay, great. Thanks."

Before Delilah made the trek uptown, she put on an extra heavy layer of powder to disguise her skin tone, making her feel like she was caked in clown makeup. She was relieved she had been dressed in the 90s vintage suit that day in the park, allowing her to wear her usual black jeans, tee, and leather jacket combo, but she worried that keeping her hood up would make it seem like she was trying *too* hard to hide her identity. Instead, she went up to Canal Street and bought a cheap Mets hat and a knockoff pair of Ray-Bans, looking every bit the aloof tourist as she hopped on the train uptown.

It was several stops later that Delilah was sure she was being followed.

She'd first noticed the man on Canal Street. He was unremarkable–a bit on the short side with an average build and one of those "Where do I know you from?" faces, dressed in dad jeans and an untucked button-down shirt–but what had got Delilah's attention wasn't how he looked but how no one else looked at him. Not a single person. Yet the Canal Street crowd managed to never bump into him, sidestepping at the last second or deciding to suddenly change direction.

Believing you're not paranoid if they're really out to get you, Delilah took a needlessly circuitous path to the train station, overtly pretending like she was being followed, complete with frequent looks around and fake relief at finding no one on her trail. Down in the belly of the station, she saw her unremarkable stalker lingering at the end of the platform while she stayed towards the middle; when the train arrived, Delilah took a seat that gave her a view of the doors that would open on her uptown-bound ride. If she really was being followed, she guessed the man would change cars at each stop, giving her four or five stops before he entered the train car she was in.

And sure enough, at Union Square she saw him walk through the doors at the back end of the car, watching him through her sunglasses while acting like she was on her phone.

Three stops later, at 33rd Street, she got off the train. It was the last station before Central Park without any line transfers. It would have to be one hell of a coincidence for Mr. Unremarkable to get off at that station and not be following Delilah. She walked slowly towards the exit as the train pulled away, spinning around just before she got to the turnstile.

There was no one there.

"How observant," said a voice from behind.

Delilah spun around again, her path to the turnstile now blocked by her stalker. Just as she'd feared–she was being followed by a fellow paranormal.

"Do I know you?" she asked. Was there an open exit on the other end of the platform in case she needed it? Delilah couldn't remember.

"I doubt it," said the man.

"Then could you please move?" she asked loudly, trying to get the attention of a couple coming down the stairs. But they didn't seem to notice Delilah or her stalker, using the turnstile next to them and then stepping around them as they strode down the platform to wait for the train.

"Don't bother," said the man. "They can't really see or hear us right now."

"Cute. I don't think I've heard of your kind before," said Delilah.

The man chuckled. "Well now, I guess you wouldn't have, would you? Me and my colleagues don't exactly keep a high profile." He held out his hand. "Ralph Ellison."

Delilah scoffed and shook the man's hand. "Really, Ralph Ellison? The writer? I think you're getting your invisible men mixed up."

"You read, good for you," Ralph said.

"Let me guess, one of your 'colleagues' is named H.G. Wells," quipped Delilah, trying to buy herself time to get a read on her stalker.

"We're all Ralph Ellison as far as the world is concerned. It keeps things cleaner."

"So, do I just call you Ralph One, Ralph Two, and so on?" asked Delilah, smirking. "Because that's *so* clean and easy."

"I wouldn't worry about it. You'd be the first to face such a... predicament." Ralph's cold, flat smile unnerved Delilah. "You too may want to consider the benefits of anonymity one day, Ms. Cruz."

Delilah narrowed her eyes at Ralph. "So is that what this is? A PSA on paranormal safety?"

Ralph's flat smile didn't flinch. "No. This is a job offer."

"No thanks."

"You haven't even heard my offer yet," said Ralph.

"Not interested," said Delilah.

"Who knows, maybe I'm offering you a position to go around saving poor defenseless trees. You seem to enjoy that."

"*Is* that the job offer?" asked Delilah. How did he know about the trees?

"Well… no," said Ralph. "But you *are* broke, apparently. And my job offer pays very well."

Delilah grumbled, hating that "Ralph Ellison" knew so much about her. Was he going to start reading her horoscope next?

"How many times do I have to tell you I'm not interested?" she asked. "I'm not some mercenary for hire. Go find one of the thousand other death witches who will gladly take your money."

"That's just it. We don't want one of the thousand other death witches. We want you. And we want you precisely because you seem so comfortable being, like I said, broke," said Ralph. "Surely you've been following the mayoral–"

"Oh not this horseshit again," said Delilah.

For the first time, Ralph's facade slipped, irritation seeping through.

"Stop being a child. If Roger Keller wins this election, no one is going to care how many trees you save or how you're 'one of the good ones' or whatever you tell yourself to get to sleep at night. They're going to come after people like you and your little girlfriend and, like me, they're going to have no problem finding you because you're both plastered all over social media. I believe you're smarter than this, Ms. Cruz. Take some time and consider working with me–we could do some real good together."

Ralph slid a business card out of his button-down pocket and handed it to Delilah. It was all black with silver lettering. On one side read "The Invisible Men" in capital letters and on the other was the name "Ralph Ellison", with a phone number underneath.

When Delilah looked up again, Ralph was gone.

"Expedited? I'm not sure that's something we've ever done," said the 50-something clerk at the GreenThumb office. She had the rounded, exhausted look of a woman ready to retire, all the edges sanded down after a lifetime of helping others.

Delilah adjusted her Mets cap, the inside chafing against her scalp. Somehow she didn't think her excuse about "peak gardening season" was going to work on a woman who worked for an organization that helped manage community gardens.

"Does that mean you can't do it?" she asked.

"Ah, I didn't say that. It's just… well, really I don't know. I guess we *could*. May I ask why you want to expedite the application process? I'm not saying I find it strange, but others might," said the clerk, her ringed auburn hair bouncing as she tilted her head to the side.

Maybe it was the clerk's exhausted look or maybe it was her encounter with "Ralph Ellison", but Delilah was tired. She didn't want to be doing this. She'd rather be in bed with Iris, lazing the day away. But then a mental image of her pale, broad frame next to Iris's petite figure flashed through her mind and she cringed with shame.

"You wanna know the truth?" asked a frustrated Delilah. "Fine, here you go: I live in a shitty apartment building in East Chinatown that my new landlord wants to sell off to be torn down because they're sad that my old landlord, their dad, is dead. Keep in mind, they're not sad about kicking everyone out on the street, but whatever. Anyway, my, uh, roommate thinks that if we can make the public garden next to our building nice, it might make our landlord reconsider. Honestly, I think that's crazy talk but I really like my roommate and I don't wanna shoot her idea down just because I don't think it'll work. *But* we only have a few weeks so I can't wait a month and a half to get approval from you guys. I have to start working on this yesterday. Is that enough of an explanation for you?'

The clerk was speechless for a few moments, her mouth hanging open. Then she said: "Let me see if I understand: You want to build out a community garden in less than a month to try to get your landlord to not sell your building."

"Yep."

"And you're doing this because it's your roommate's idea, who you 'really like' and who you don't want to disappoint."

"Yep."

"What happens if you build out this garden and your landlord still sells your building?" the clerk asked.

Delilah shrugged. "I guess we'll have somewhere nice to sleep when we're homeless then," said Delilah jokingly.

The clerk didn't seem amused. She pursed her lips, thinking, and after a few heavy moments of consideration said: "You must have some roommate if you'd stick it out together homeless too. Let's hope it doesn't come to that. I am going to look into expediting your application but do me a favor–come up with a story that's going to be easier for my bosses to swallow. Maybe say you want to have the garden ready for summer or something. June, maybe. You could say it's for Pride, assuming you and your–" The clerk cleared her throat. "–roommate celebrate."

It was then that Delilah noticed the rainbow pin camouflaged on the clerk's colorful blouse. She laughed to herself, thinking how much easier this could've been had she just calmed down.

"Thank you," Delilah said softly.

"My pleasure," said the clerk. She passed over a packet of forms and took down Delilah's email. "Fill these out and I'll schedule a review meeting as soon as I can, hopefully in the next day or two."

"Perfect, will do. Thank you again," said Delilah as she collected the papers.

The clerk smiled wistfully and asked, "What's your roommate's name, by the way?"

"Iris," said Delilah, surprisingly proud to speak her name aloud.

"That's a pretty name. I'll be pulling for you."

As Delilah left the GreenThumb office, she put her sunglasses back on, remembering what Stavros had said earlier in the week: *If this election goes south, we paras are going to need all the allies we can get.*

It was nice to have allies. Though somewhere deep inside, Delilah knew it was even nicer not to need them.

Toil & Trouble

~IRIS~

That night, the witches shared the headway they had made over baked mac and cheese, Iris cooking it the way Nanna Anna always did: a little cream of tartar, Velveeta, and 4C breadcrumbs. She wanted to make it with the okra and spinach sides too, but Iris couldn't bring herself to cook up fresh vegetables, not even for Delilah.

Things were going well it seemed–Delilah had found a way to get their garden application fast tracked and Iris had already called the Department of Sanitation, who said they'd send a truck over the next day to haul out the trash, no permits needed. But Iris didn't tell Delilah about her run-in with Marco, deciding it was for the best not to upset her. They both seemed to have let the encounter go–for now–and Iris feared that if Delilah found out about her run-in, she'd go knocking on doors until she figured out where he lived. Better to keep moving forward and avoid ticking off their neighbors even more, as the Basilisk had advised them.

The witches agreed to sleep in their own rooms that night, Iris feeling bad that she'd left Philly, Carl, and the rest of her potted plants all alone. But around five in the morning, when the morning light was beginning to trickle in through the windows, Iris woke up. She'd expected to be missing the feel of Delilah next to her, but she was uneasy with how okay she was with it; after the night they'd shared, shouldn't Iris be yearning for more? Shouldn't she want to feel the pale witch under her fingers again? She knew part of her was being ridiculous, but Iris feared the green witch in her was driving her away from Delilah.

It was enough to drag Iris out of bed and into Delilah's room, not caring that she had left her wig behind. She slinked in bed next to Delilah, the other woman stirring awake in a half daze and pulling Iris close before falling asleep again, cradling Iris in the crook of her arm. There was no patchouli perfume cover-up fragrance masking Delilah's natural scent, allowing Iris to breathe in the death witch's earthy, strong aroma as she too drifted back to sleep.

When she woke again at ten to seven, Delilah was coming back into the bedroom. Seeing Iris's eyes open, the witch hurried back under the covers like she was ashamed to be seen naked. It shouldn't have bothered Iris as much as it did but having someone who'd spent nearly forty minutes between Iris's legs be so shy about her own body struck a nerve. Had that been it, Iris would've let it go. But there was more. As Iris cuddled up to Delilah there was a new smell, neither her natural scent nor the heavy patchouli. No, this was sweet and floral and it made Iris's nostrils itch.

"What is that?" whispered Iris.

"What?" asked Delilah.

"Why do you smell different?" asked Iris.

"It's a new perfume," Delilah said. "I got it yesterday. I wanted to… try it out."

"At seven in the morning?

Delilah went silent, looking up at the still vine-covered ceiling, mulling over her next words.

"What's with you and smells?" she finally asked, defensively.

"What's with *you* and smells?" Iris shot back.

"I just wanted to smell nice for you," pouted Delilah. "I didn't know you'd come into my bed in the middle of the night." Her voice was so uncharacteristically tiny and hurt that it snapped Iris out of her annoyance.

Iris nuzzled against Delilah, feeling the tight rise and fall of her chest. She drew the pads of her fingertips along the other witch's cool skin with idle strokes, tracing imaginary circles and triangles and other shapes.

"I'll keep saying this as long as it takes to sink in," said Iris. "I like the way you smell."

Although Iris was hoping that would get Delilah to relax, the pale witch retreated into herself again. Even though she had her eyes closed, Iris could tell from Delilah's breathing that she was still wide awake.

Iris woke yet again at eight thirty, not sure if Delilah had ever made it back to sleep. She kissed Delilah on the cheek and went to get up out of bed, but Delilah wrapped her arm around her waist, pulling her close to whisper in her ear.

"Do you want to help me wash this perfume off?" whispered Delilah.

Even though it sounded like Delilah had been waiting to use that line for the last hour and a half, Iris's heart skipped a beat. The rush of adrenaline made her say something back that surprised herself.

"Only if you promise to let me do all the washing."

Delilah wrapped her legs around Iris's waist and wrestled her onto her back, pinning Iris's shoulders with her hands. Her pale blues eyes gazed down at Iris and Iris could feel Delilah fighting hard to not hide her naked body.

Her heart racing excitedly, Iris made a dramatic sniffing motion. "You *stink*," she teased. "Let me go get the shower ready so we can scrub all that cloying perfume off that beautiful skin."

Delilah let Iris up and Iris went off to the bathroom, bringing the candles from their coffee table with her. She let the shower run hot and lit the candles so that the shower was dim and steamy by the time she called for Delilah.

"Shower's ready," she said.

Delilah stepped into the bathroom anxiously, easing up once she realized how dark it was in there. Iris peaked around the shower curtain.

"Ready when you are," said Iris.

Through the thickening steam and dim candlelight, Iris could just see Delilah's tall, alabaster frame step into the shower. Her arms were rigid at her side, like her hands were fighting a magnetic force to cover up her body.

"Face the showerhead," said Iris, feeling possessed with a confidence she'd never known before. It was how she expected someone like Delilah to act, not her–but there was something about such a strong, intimidating woman being shy around Iris that made her own strength blossom.

Iris picked up her moss-colored poofy loofah sponge and squeezed out a heavy dollop of moisturizing body wash on it, lathering it in her hands and then rubbing it against Delilah's upper back in soft, long strokes from her neck towards her arms.

"You're so much taller than me," Iris said, her mouth taking on more and more a mind of its own. "Maybe I should make you get on your knees."

Delilah's voice was tight with excitement. "I can get on my knees," she said.

"Maybe later," mused Iris, bringing the loofah down Delilah's back.

Iris washed the witch all the way down to her waist, using one hand to hold Delilah steady by her hip. She made small, deep circles along Delilah's ass, lathering one cheek and then the other, and then left Delilah with a soapy backside as she pretended to lather her loofah again. Through the curling steam, she admired how the thick, bubbly soap traced its way along Delilah's curves and down her thighs, enjoying that almost as much as she enjoyed how obediently Delilah waited for Iris to continue.

Who am *I?* thought Iris giddily, having never been one to take control of a situation.

She remembered how peaceful she had felt in the garden that morning and how she had thought it was even more peaceful than her time with Delilah. Now she felt the complete opposite. Which was the real high for Iris?

Not now, thought Iris. *Enjoy this. Focus on this.*

Iris brought the loofah back to Delilah's ass and in a shameful, lusty little move brought it right down between the death witch's cheeks. Delilah flinched.

"Just making sure you're nice and clean," said Iris. She knelt down in the shower, sitting back on her heels, and adoringly washed Delilah's long legs. From behind, she scrubbed her way up the witch's shins and knees and thighs, getting closer and closer to that warm valley between her legs. Iris was amused by how Delilah instinctively inched her hips back at the touch of the loofah, inadvertently bumping her taut bottom against Iris's face and apologizing with adorable shyness. Iris had to resist the heady urge to kiss and nibble the soft, pale skin in front of her, getting needy and squirmy herself.

"Okay, turn around so we can wash the soap off–and so I can scrub the rest of you down," said Iris.

Without the thick steam, Iris wasn't sure Delilah would've turned towards her so easily, her arms still held stiffly at her sides. She seemed to stiffen up even more when she realized Iris was the one on her knees with her face in Delila's crotch, but the misty veil seemed enough to keep Delilah from freaking out.

"Did you spray that perfume here?" asked Iris, touching the V between Delilah's legs tenderly with the loofah.

"I don't remember," said Delilah. Her voice was tense, but she was trying so hard to play into their little game that Iris couldn't help but be delighted.

"No point taking risks," said Iris as she pressed the loofah against Delilah.

The death witch let out a deep sigh.

"I don't think this is going to be enough," said Iris suggestively. She held up the loofah sponge. "Hold this, please."

Delilah finally had to peel her arms off her sides to take the sponge from Iris. She seemed to hold it strategically, blocking Iris from her misty view–and letting Iris get a tender look at Delilah's sex. Through the flickering light and steamy air, she took in the sight of Delilah, the intimate folds pale and ashen much like the rest of the witch. But her lips were like Delilah's mouth and nipples–a dark, deep purple-black that reminded Iris of an exotic tulip.

She touched her tongue to Delilah's dripping, warm flower. Immediately, Delilah's thighs tensed and then slowly relaxed as Iris brought her tongue up to Delilah's dark violet pearl. It was stiff already. Delilah let out an even deeper sigh, her fingers kneading the loofah sponge. Iris licked again, more daringly this time, her tongue slipping past Delilah's wet, black plum lips. The death witch gasped.

"Am I dirty in there too?" Delilah joked with a nervous laugh.

"This might be the dirtiest place yet," said Iris, diving her tongue in deeper. She tasted everything Delilah seemed so upset and unsure about, lapping her tongue against a deep, rich fragrance well of leather and oil and myrrh and saffron. How could this woman ever be ashamed of her body? She was everything Iris wasn't–strong, powerful, bold.

The warm spray of the shower rained down on Iris as she grasped Delilah's legs to steady herself, sucking gently on Delilah's lips and making the tall woman moan. Iris loved

Delilah's sounds and the tensing of her body as the green witch danced her mouth along her, like she was playing some beautiful, magnificent instrument. As Iris wrapped her lips around Delilah's stiffened dark pearl, the loofah fell, bouncing off of Iris's head and onto the shower floor.

Pulling her mouth away from Delilah for a moment, Iris tut-tutted. "Are you trying to tell me you're wet enough and that you don't need that anymore?" she asked.

Delilah responded only with deep, sighing breaths.

"In that case…" said Iris.

She wrapped her plush lips around Delilah again, using just the tip of her tongue to please the woman towering above her. Delilah, overwhelmed with the sensation, took a step back, her body pressing against the tiled wall; Iris moved with her, the shower pouring down on both of them at once. Up above, Iris could see Delilah's hands moving through the steam as she tried to figure out what to do with them, clenching her fingers and looking for something–anything–to grab onto.

Iris was reeling with the power she felt over Delilah. She brought her hands around and, as Iris tongued Delilah's pearl, she slid two fingers inside of the witch, working them to the rhythm of her licking. Delilah's hands slapped against the wet tile wall and very softly she whispered, "Fuck yes."

They moved as one under the water, Iris's head and hand bobbing between Delilah's legs, Delilah sliding up and down against the tile. More husky moaning words of arousal escaped Delilah–"Yes, fuck, oh fuck fuck fuck, oh god, oh yes"–and Iris felt the muscles in the other witch's thighs flex and clench along with her toes that curled against Iris's knees. Iris turned her hand palm-up, making a "come hither" motion with her fingers to please Delilah from the inside.

Delilah's body began to shake. Just as Iris thought she was on the verge of bubbling over into orgasm, Delilah reached her hands down and gently but firmly pulled Iris's head away. She looked at Iris through the steam, pale cheeks practically pink and her chest heaving.

"I wasn't done," said Iris, her fingers still deep in Delilah's warmth.

"We'll finish later, okay?" said Delilah.

She put a hand on Iris's wrist, guiding the green witch out of her. Iris didn't get it. Had she done something wrong?

"Uh, okay," Iris said, trying hard not to show her disappointment.

"You can still, you know, finish washing," said Delilah, tripping over her own words. "Or I can…"

"No no, you promised you'd let me do all the washing," said Iris.

But her heart was no longer in it. She finished sponging down Delilah and rinsed her off, letting the tall woman out of the shower first so Iris could frown without Delilah seeing.

By now, Delilah's self-consciousness was obvious, but Iris was running out of ways to tell Delilah that she didn't care about the issues Delilah had with her body, she just wanted her for her. After the shower, they dressed, Delilah in another one of her nondescript black-jeans-white-tee combos and Iris in a pink satiny romper dress. Its scandalously short hem and spaghetti straps were meant to get Delilah's attention, but she seemed so focused on covering herself up that she barely seemed to notice before she was off to work.

"Why don't you give me the garden paperwork to do?" asked Iris. "I'll be just hanging around here anyway."

"It's fine," said Delilah. "I know you don't like paper. Plus, my bar's not like Anyway Bar, the day shifts are slow as shit. I can do it there, no one will care."

"Maybe I can swing by and say hi," said Iris.

"It's really awful there during the day. Trust me, you don't want to be there, it's just old people and alcoholics," said Delilah, glancing away.

"Alright…" It took everything Iris had not to turn their goodbye into a fight.

Delilah gave Iris a kiss on the cheek. "Maybe you can work on the social media stuff? You could do before and after videos before they come clean out the garden lot."

"Yeah. Okay," said Iris.

Once Delilah was off to work, Iris went into her bedroom and sat surrounded by her potted plants, begging them to tell her how she could get Delilah to stop being so afraid of her own body. But the plants had no answers for that kind of dilemma, the only things on their photosynthesizing minds was how much sun, rich soil, and freedom they could get to grow unimpeded.

~DELILAH~

Stupid, stupid, stupid. What's wrong with me? Why didn't I let her keep going?

That was the thought that ran through Delilah's head during her day shift at the bar. Compared to Anyway Bar, which was grimy but at least had personality–and witches–Delilah's bar had none of the personality, none of the witches, and twice the grime. It was called "McManus" even though it wasn't remotely Irish and half the people who came during the day shift seemed like they'd already been drinking elsewhere and the other half seemed like they were on their way to somewhere else. The only saving grace about the dump was that no one gave a fuck that Delilah was a death witch.

She stared at the still-blank GreenThumb paperwork, unable to stop thinking about Iris. The entire morning had been a disaster: more than a hundred bucks wasted on that J'adore perfume, an amazing shower together ruined by Delilah's hangups, and to top it all off, Delilah giving Iris the cold shoulder before work. And now it seemed like she was going to make it even worse by not doing the one thing she said she'd do, the dumb, stupid paperwork.

At least Claire, the clerk from GreenThumb, had emailed her to let her know she could come in tomorrow morning to review the application–assuming she could get off her ass and do it– and that it would more than likely be approved without issue.

Delilah poured herself a shot of cheap house whiskey. She opened up TikTok and looked up the account Iris had made, Two_Broke_Witches. Iris had already posted twenty videos– twenty!–in a bunch of meme formats. Flipping through them, Delilah cringed at the dramatic looks on her face as she held her palms out to the trees, but Iris had done an amazing job getting nice shots and splicing together videos into quick, snappy clips. As she watched, a stream of comments floated up from the bottom of the screen:

"This is so fake lololol. She probably threatened whoever filmed this."

"I don't care if she's trying to do good, I wouldn't trust her with MY life."

"Death witches are the worst lmao."

"i never thought i'd be rooting for the lanternflies but dayam here i am"

"She's only doing this for attention and followers, DWs be manipulative af."

Delilah groaned. "Fucking great," she said.

Then just before she closed the app, one more comment floated up.

"I get what she's trying to do but…"

It was from a_human_laywer, the woman who doled out legal advice for non-paras, and there was a response video attached. Delilah clicked into the comments and played the video low on her phone so that the drunks at the bar wouldn't hear. A prim blonde in a dark blazer with muted makeup filled the screen.

"I get what she's trying to do but this is why we have a Parks Department. It's why we have professional exterminators. We can't just have paras with their privileged powers running around doing whatever they want. What if there had been other animals in this tree? Imagine a family of squirrels or some newly hatched baby birds–would we have seen those on this video? Of course not. Look, I don't want to put witches or any other paranormal down unfairly, but the sheer power this witch has should terrify you. This behavior needs regulation and the paras aren't going to regulate themselves. If the federal government won't step in, then we need local government to–and that means we need Roger Keller as New York's next mayor or soon enough there won't be room left for us normal folks anymore."

Delilah's blood boiled.

She looked towards the GreenThumb paperwork, knowing she should put her phone away and get to it. But instead she searched for the hashtag "deathwitch" on TikTok and got sucked into a doomscroll of people hating on death witches. Most of them were people memeing the wealthy socialite celebrity death witches, like Lady Cassandra and Glinda Gorgon, but the more Delilah scrolled, the more she saw videos of women–seemingly only women, oddly enough–breaking down what they called the "DBL", or the "death bitch look". They pointed out how death witches had long faces and strong noses and mannish jawlines, comparing them to old fairytale drawings of ugly trolls and goblins.

One achingly beautiful brunette whispered conspiratorially

to the camera: "Do we think death witches even have sex? I mean, I'm sure *someone* is into them but that is… yikes."

That was enough for Delilah. She put her phone down and went to the bathroom, not sure if she wanted to cry or beat her fist against the wall until she bled.

~IRIS~

Iris couldn't believe it when the Department of Sanitation showed up at noon on the dot. She watched through her bedroom window as four men hopped out of the truck and began hauling the junk in the garden lot away like it was just another trash pickup. Part of her wanted to run out and thank them–maybe even hug them–but Iris stopped herself. She'd already had one encounter in the lot and didn't want to cause another should anyone else be watching.

Seed shopping was next on Iris's list. Home Depot's Garden Center didn't have the best selection, but they were certainly the cheapest for what they had. Iris lost herself browsing the store, walking up and down the aisles and sliding her hand across little plastic boxes stuffed with seed packets.

Seeds didn't communicate the way grown plants did, but nevertheless there were little signs of which ones would grow the best and most harmoniously–bumpy vibrations, tiny specks of color in Iris's vision–which allowed Iris to gather two dozen packets that already felt like a floral family. There was purple butterfly bush, striking red bee balm, daisy-like black-eyed Susans, scratchy milkweed, pink asters, cornflowers, hydrangeas that would bloom cobalt blue and deep lavender in the lot, and many more, the assortment sure to be colorful and varied.

As she was getting ready to leave, she overheard two middle-aged women with tourist accents laughing by the escalators.

"This is just sad," one said to the other, feeling a fern between her fingers, nearly ripping a leaf off. "Almost thirty dollars for this. Imagine living in this concrete zoo and having to pay this much for a dang fern."

"Oh if you think that's bad, I saw some poor girl picking out seed packets like she was at a toy store."

"The one with the pink hair?"

"That's her alright."

The women laughed.

"I bet the sorry little thing's never lived nowhere else," the first woman said.

"Prolly doesn't even know those flowers grow naturally," the other woman said.

They laughed again.

Iris stayed hidden, waiting for them to leave before she went upstairs and paid for her basket of seed packets. Back out on the street, Iris felt nauseous having spent so much time in the crowded Home Depot, rushing as fast as he could to get away from the swarms of people walking up and down the block. The women's laughter echoed in her ears.

~DELILAH~

On her way home from the dull day shift, Delilah made a stop at a nearby bodega's florist picking out a bright white calla lily for Iris, having read about them while at work. It was an eye-popping $25 for a bodega plant, but Delilah wanted to make amends for the crummy morning and to show Iris she'd been thinking of her. At home though, Iris was asleep in bed with her door closed; Delilah left the lily of Iris's door and started on dinner.

Delilah wasn't much of a cook but she knew a few recipes. Avoiding any leafy plants that would unsettle Iris, she put together a mushroom risotto with plenty of butter, cheese, and shallots, skipping the chives and other green bits. The dish turned out creamy and savory, and Delilah remembered how much she loved the earthy aroma of mushrooms.

Funny, I like beets too, she thought. *And carrots and potatoes and turnips…*

Everything earthy and dirty. Delilah laughed to herself. *Go figure.* Cooking helped her not think about her earlier doomscrolling, though the sips from her refilled flask might've contributed to that. She poured a splash of whiskey into the risotto, thinking it might impart some woodiness to the mushrooms.

Iris's door creaked open.

"What's this?" she asked groggily, picking up the potted flower.

"Oh, that's for you," said Delilah. "I saw it and thought you might like it."

"A calla lily," Iris said flatly.

"Is it no good? I tried my best to get something I thought you'd like," said Delilah.

Iris rubbed her eyes. "No, no, it's just… Maddy is antisocial. She gets very territorial."

"Maddy?"

"Ah, sorry," said Iris. "Maddy is my Madonna lily. The white star-shaped flower in my room."

"Oh."

Iris sniffed at the air, eager to change the topic. "Did you make dinner?"

"I did! Mushroom risotto with Parmesan and shallots. No greens, don't worry," Delilah said proudly.

"Mushrooms?" asked Iris.

"You can eat mushrooms, right…?"

Iris looked down at the potted calla lily in her hands, twisting her lips to the side. "I try not to. But it's okay, I can find something else to eat."

"Really?" said an exasperated Delilah. She was so close to telling Iris about her doomscrolling, only stopping because she didn't want the green witch to feel bad about posting the videos of Delilah's tree cleansing to TikTok.

"I mean, like, I don't feel as close to fungi as plants, but it's still tough for me," said Iris. "I can hear them, if I try."

"I didn't know." Delilah could no longer hide her annoyance.

"It's okay, really. You should still enjoy it–it smells amazing."

"What are you going to eat?" asked Delilah.

"I'll just have leftovers."

And so they ate, Delilah with her risotto she'd cooked for Iris, Iris with the baked mac and cheese she'd cooked for Delilah, and the potted calla lily in front of them. They swapped their tiny wins for the day–the paperwork, the junkyard cleanup–but the simmering tension between them on the saggy loveseat made it obvious that was not what they really wanted to share.

"I'm sorry about freaking out this morning"–that's what Delilah wanted to say. But even though she ran up the courage to share the feeling with Iris again and again, she couldn't bring herself to say the words out loud. Out of the corner of her eye, she watched the beautiful, glowing green witch eat her mac and cheese while not even glancing at the calla lily and Delilah wondered why she was so shitty at this. She was good at flirting and at fucking–as long as she was giving–but when it came to everything after, she was a failure. Maybe it was in her death witch blood, some hard coded calamity that made sure she would never get close to anyone so she could fulfill her genetic destiny to kill, kill, kill.

Later, after both witches were done with their food and had whittled away a few hours on their phones, Delilah asked Iris if she wanted to go to Anyway Bar.

"Now?" asked Iris, looking at the time on her phone. "It's getting close to ten. Didn't you say it gets bad then?"

"Not always," said Delilah.

"I don't know… I don't think it's a good idea for me to drink tonight," said Iris. "I want to start planting seeds first thing tomorrow morning. But you can go if you want and, like, do your usual thing."

Was there something in Iris's voice? An insinuation or accusation, as if Delilah might go to Anyway Bar and find some other witch to admire? She bristled at the idea that Iris was somehow better than her for wanting to pass up any chance to have fun so she could wake up early and work.

"Nah, I think you've got the right idea–I should do the same and bring this paperwork back. As long as we get it approved tomorrow, I don't think anyone is going to mind that you started planting seeds early," said Delilah. She swallowed hard. "Wanna cuddle for a bit? Maybe in your room this time?"

"Okay," said Iris.

The two witches lied side by side, looking at the creeper vines that had covered Iris's room since the day they'd moved in. Unlike the ones in Delilah's room that had just come in a few days ago, these seemed somehow snooty, like they were turning away every time Delilah glanced at them. Even though the women were holding hands and touching their feet together, Delilah knew neither she nor Iris was fully there, their minds far away.

"I'm excited for the garden," said Delilah, trying to push out thoughts about the nasty TikTok comments.

"Me too," said Iris.

Delilah tried to sleep but couldn't.

BURNING BRIDGES

~DELILAH~

True to her word, Iris was up at the crack of dawn to plant seeds. She gave Delilah a kiss on the cheek and got dressed while Delilah–pretending to still be asleep–watched her put on dark denim overalls and a green blouse with flounce sleeves, along with a white bucket hat in lieu of her wig. Seeing Iris's radiant, curvy body filled Delilah with adoration–along with a nagging jealousy. No matter how much Delilah powdered or bronzed her face or switched up her style or vowed not to use her death magick, she would never, ever look like Iris. Or Ruth. Or any of the other witches she'd hooked up with in her life and then ran away from in the light of day.

Delilah could see the green witch working in the garden lot through the bedroom window. She seemed so… happy, at peace in a way Delilah hadn't seen her before. Hell, at peace in a way *Delilah* had never been before. Iris spent long stretches deliberating where to sprinkle seeds, walking back and forth across the overgrown lot without a care in the world.

It must be nice, she thought. *To be a witch with an affinity you can indulge in without hurting anyone.*

As much as she hated to admit it, maybe there was something to green witches living in the wilderness after all.

While Iris worked, Delilah got ready for the day, slipping out before Iris came back. She had to bring the GreenThumb paperwork back to the Central Park office, but first she had to make a phone call.

"And why would I have heard of these people?" asked Stavros Basil on the other end of the line. Even though it was a quarter to eight, he sounded like he'd been up for hours.

"You're the biggest para-lawyer in town," said Delilah. "Are you really telling me you've *never* crossed paths with the Invisible Men?"

Stavros hmmed. "I did tell you DWEs were always in demand," he said smugly. "An offer from the Invisible Men though, that's… that's something else."

"Is it legit?" Delilah asked.

"As in, will they actually pay you and not betray you? In that case, yes, it's legit," said Stavros.

"What about in the other cases?"

There was silence on the line and for a few moments Delilah thought Stavros had hung up on her.

"I'm not their spokesperson Ms. Cruz and I'm not in a position to divulge the full extent of what I know. Attorney-client privilege and whatnot. But let me just say this: some jobs require more passion than others and the Invisible Men are a passionate bunch. Do you understand?"

Not really, but I doubt you're going to get any less cryptic, thought Delilah.

"Yeah, got it," she said.

Having still an hour before the GreenThumb office opened, Delilah decided to walk up from East Chinatown, once again in her Mets cap and sunglasses. It was one of those mid-spring mornings that felt like winter had never left and a nasty wind whipped down 5th Avenue; Delilah hoped that Iris had finished her planting and was inside already. They had twenty days left before their eviction, but Delilah worried she and Iris were spiraling out of control–Stavros had been no help, social media had been a bust, and the idea of using a garden to make nice with their neighbors was beginning to feel like wishful thinking at best.

Delilah should've said something sooner. But she hadn't because she was enjoying their camaraderie. No, that wasn't it. Well, sure, Delilah did enjoy working alongside Iris but that hadn't kept Delilah's mouth shut, the fear of upsetting Iris did.

Had it been anyone else, Delilah would've already said what a doomed, naive plan this was, but Delilah was terrified that if she said that to Iris then all of a sudden all of Iris's soothing words about liking Delilah's body would go up in smoke.

A gust of wind caught Delilah in the face and tore her Mets cap off, sending it tumbling into the street. It landed in an iridescent puddle of motor oil and who knew what else.

Fuck it, she thought. *I don't need it.*

She stubbornly walked the rest of the way, spitefully passing by every subway station until she'd reached the GreenThumb office. The clerk with the ringed auburn hair wasn't there and Delilah was directed to wait at her desk for someone to review her forms.

A man with brushed back messy hair and a beard took a seat across from Delilah. When he saw her, he nearly spilled his coffee on his lap.

"You…" he said.

It was one of the park workers from after their meeting with the Basilisk.

"Oh shit," said Delilah, unable to help herself.

The man started to stand back up.

"Wait, wait, wait," said Delilah. "I'm not here to cause trouble. I just want to get this community garden application reviewed."

"Yeah, that's what Claire said. And I thought it was gonna be cut and dry but this changes everything lady," the bearded man said.

"What? Why? Because I'm a witch?" Delilah asked, her tone accusatory.

"No, because I'm not normally the guy who reviews these. I was just doing this because my boss is running late. And you've already met him. He's not exactly your biggest fan."

The memory of the old, leathery man with the chainsaw pointed at Iris was all too clear.

"*He's* in charge of this?" asked Delilah, stunned.

The bearded man nodded apologetically. "For like twenty years now. If you weren't, uh, you, then I think he'd happily approve it. But this is dead in the water, I'm sorry."

"Can't you just approve it quickly before he gets here?" asked Delilah, pushing the paperwork towards the man. "What's the harm in doing that? It's a goddamn community garden."

Just then, Delilah's phone chimed with an incoming email. She thought she'd put her phone on silent mode to block out the constant cookie cutter job offers, but as she looked at her phone's glowing screen, she saw the email was marked urgent. The subject line read: *Important - You Have Been Named in a Civil Suit.*

FUCK!

"I really can't, if my boss finds out I approved it for yo–"

Delilah slammed her fist down on the table. "Stop being such a pussy!" she growled. "Your boss is a miserable bigot who is going to reject my application because I stopped him from threatening my goddamn–" Delilah struggled for the next word. Partner? Lover? Girlfriend? " –roommate with a chainsaw and you're too chickenshit to stand up to him."

The bearded man held up his hands in self-defense. "Ma'am, I'm going to need to ask you to leave now," he said.

Delilah huffed a bitter laugh and felt the start of tears in her eyes. "I really am a piece of shit, huh?" she said to no one. As she looked at the bearded man, a hot tear streaked down her cheek. "I'm sorry. I know it's not your fault, I'm just… having a bad life is all." She slid the paperwork over to him. "You can keep this. Throw it out if you want, give it to your boss to wipe his ass on, whatever. I don't fucking care anymore."

She could feel the eyes of the other office workers on her as she dragged her ass out of the building, weighed down by the thought that she had just killed Iris's dumb, naive, beautiful plan for a garden.

~IRIS~

Iris stared numbly at her phone. But what was numbing her wasn't the email confirming that she and Delilah were in fact being sued for hundreds of thousands of dollars, but that Delilah hadn't called or texted Iris to even talk about it.

At first, Iris figured Delilah had just been busy or that maybe she'd had her phone off. That thought was a consolation for the first two hours. However, when she still hadn't heard from Delilah five hours later, Iris started to unravel.

There's no way she hasn't seen this yet, she thought. *What is she doing? Is she okay? Are* we *okay?*

Iris had gone from waiting in her room to waiting in the garden lot, hidden by a tall patch of ragweed. She both hated and loved how safe she felt amongst the vegetation and the new seedlings that had already begun to sprout thanks to her green magick. She tapped out text after text to Delilah, deleting them before sending–she was tired of being the one doing the chasing, of trying to prove to herself that she might not wind up alone and all the happier for it. Iris wanted to be chased and pursued and…

Loved.

Was there something about her being a green witch that repelled people? Something that made people on some primal, instinctual level realize Iris was not *supposed* to be around other people? Is that what happened with her parents? Even before Iris started treating plants like "imaginary friends" and her petal hair started growing in, did her parents somehow just know what she was and start taking up their vices to push themselves away from her?

Iris heard the rustling sound of footsteps through grass and held her breath. Was it Delilah? Had she come looking for her?

As a lavender flame ignited twenty feet away and quickly spread, Iris knew it was not Delilah. No, this flame wasn't just lavender–it was bright orange too, a *real* flame. A plume of smoke began to rise in the air.

No! My seedlings!

Iris bolted up from the ragweed. Standing next to the spreading fire was Marco, once again wearing his black ski mask. When he noticed her, he gave her a panicked look.

"I didn't think anyone would be here," he said, dumbfounded. "You shouldn't have been here!"

The fire leapt from the grass to the dry weeds, ripping through the back half of the lot, carried by the windy weather. Iris could feel the plant life screaming shrilly and then going grimly silent. Marco took off running, but Iris didn't even think about chasing him–she was too disoriented by the screaming plants and the billowing heat of the fire to think straight.

"No, no no no," she said, eyes searching the ground for any seedlings she might be able to save.

There was too much smoke. As Iris breathed it in, she realized she needed to get out of there, immediately. She took off running to the edge of the lot, away from the fire, but was stopped by the lot's seven-foot-tall wrought iron fence. Where were the exits? There were two, she remembered, but with the seedlings, grass, and weeds crying out and the smoke thickening, Iris couldn't orient herself. A siren blared in the distance; it sounded far away. Her heart pounded as she realized what she had to do.

She had to climb the fence.

Her legs trembling and hands shaking, Iris clambered onto the fence, using its wrought iron detailing as a foothold. The plant screams were deafening now as the rest of the garden's vegetation awaited their fate. She turned over her shoulder and saw the fire was winding its way around the edge of the lot, using the dead vines wrapped around the fence as kindling. With a feeling like a knife in her heart, Iris lifted her foot onto a tangle of vines and climbed up to the top of the fence, trying not to skewer herself on its pickets. Weeds and little offshoots woven through the dead vines begged Iris to help them, but she could do nothing.

The green witch threw herself over the fence and landed on the sidewalk so hard it knocked the wind out of her. Once she'd caught her breath, Iris took off running, having no idea where she was going, only that she had to get away from the fire before anyone took a video of her there.

Was that Marco's plan? To make it look like *she* had set the fire? Why?

Iris ran for five blocks before the smoke in her lungs made her stop and double over in a coughing fit. She went to text Delilah–there was no point being moody anymore–and realized that she must have dropped her phone in the garden lot. Any other time Iris would've broke down crying in the street. But not today.

Today, she was furious.

She'd lost her seedlings. The garden lot was torched, maybe even the apartment she was trying to save and all her plants in it. New York City itself seemed to be trying to expel her like she was a virus. And Delilah, the witch she'd admired for the last year and who had made her feel like no one else ever had, seemed to have put up her own fence between her and Iris.

All Iris wanted was to be close to someone, and at every turn fate, destiny, or whatever the hell you wanted to call it seemed all too happy to deny her again and again and again.

You want to get rid of me, New York? Fine. I'll let you do your worst. But I'm not backing down this time.

Iris marched to the closest subway stop she could find. It didn't matter which one, because she was going to the densest, most crowded place in New York: Times Square.

~DELILAH~

Coffin House was more than a bar. Even though it couldn't technically ban everyone but death witches and their male equivalents–stone lords–the atmosphere it created did just that, turning the dark, elegant establishment in the bowels of Grand Central Station into a kind of social club for New York's wealthiest, most hated paranormal demographic. At any other bar with marble countertops and crystal chandeliers, Delilah would've looked and been treated like a bum, but at Coffin House there were no snide looks or whispered gossip. She took a seat at the bar and ordered a Manhattan.

"Choice of whiskey, Miss?" asked the tuxedoed bartender. For a moment, Delilah thought he was the only non-para in the place until she realized the inky shadows of Coffin House were hiding his stone lord features.

"Something nice. How about… Weller 12," said Delilah, her laugh drunken despite being completely sober. "I'm celebrating."

The stone lord gave her a private grin. "Oh? What's the occasion?"

"New job," said Delilah. She set her phone and Ralph Ellison's business card on the marble bartop.

"Congratulations," said the bartender. "Let me get you the right accouterment to celebrate with."

When the stone lord stepped away to make Delilah's drink, she texted the number on the business card:

"I'm in. But I want a signing bonus. I don't know how much, but it's gotta be enough to relocate me, my roommate, and pay some hefty legal fees. Take it or leave it."

Delilah felt *good*. Finally, she'd flung that dark little door in her heart wide open and simply stopped caring. Her parents monetized her, her neighbors hated her, strangers on the internet wanted people like he exiled or worse. And Iris…

"And Iris will be much happier without me," she said.

"What was that?" asked the stone lord bartender as he set Delilah's Manhattan down, its glass looking like it cost more than Delilah made in an entire shift at McManus and Style Revival combined.

"Nothing." She held up her glass to the bartender. "Cheers."

He nodded politely and stepped down the bar to help another customer.

"Who's Iris?" asked a woman two seats down. She was in her late forties or early fifties, wearing a black frill dress, a lapis lazuli necklace, and a black sun hat with a curved brim. Her skin was even more pale than Delilah's, though it might have just been the bright crimson lipstick she wore that made it seem that way.

"Nobody," said Delilah, in no mood to talk about it.

"Not a death witch then," the woman said. "Because every death witch is a somebody." She took a sip from her champagne flute, a full bottle of something expensive-looking kept on a bucket of ice on the bar for her. "What's your new job? Let me guess, you're going to grunt and dodge my question."

Delilah had to chuckle at that. "I seem that friendly, huh?"

"Hmmm. Beat-up jeans. Old jacket. New job. I'm guessing you've never been here before," the woman said. "This place brings out the unfriendly until you get used to it. And then it brings out something much, much more delectable."

"And what's that?"

"That wonderful, smug feeling of superiority that you *belong* here." The woman extended a thin hand. "Nikka."

Delilah shook the woman's hand. "Delilah."

Her phone buzzed to life with a text back from the number on the card:

"Deal. We'll be in touch."

"So, that job of yours… I'm sorry, I don't mean to pry. I guess it's just one of the downsides of early retirement," said Nikka.

"I think it's probably best if I don't talk about it," said Delilah.

"Ah, so real DWE work. No wonder you're celebrating. I spent fifteen years in the private sector myself, mostly Finance, a few Biotech firms. I believe my title was 'Mediation Consultant.'" Nikka barked a laugh. "I made them a lot of money and in return they gave a lot of it back to me. Not a bad way to do business."

Delilah sipped her Manhattan, wishing a little bit that she'd just ordered the whiskey neat instead. "But paras don't own those firms I'm sure," she said. "Aren't you worried that those CEOs are donors for assholes like Keller?"

Nikka scoffed, dismissing Delilah's concerns. "People are getting entirely too worked up about him. I know I'm getting five or six emails a day from Coven Hub trying to drum up panic."

"So you don't think he'll try to deport paras?" asked Delilah.

"That's the thing, it doesn't matter," said Nikka.

"How so?"

"Because we're death witches," Nikka said, like she was a frustrated teacher trying to explain something to a slow student. "Death witches, stone lords, seers… there's a whole bunch of us who are just too valuable to deport. Worst comes to worst, he'll institute a visa system or something that will be trivial for us."

"So you think he's going to win?" asked Delilah.

"Darling, do you ever lift your head out of those drinks of yours? He's pretty much already won," said Nikka.

"But the election isn't for six months…"

"Ah to be young and naive," said Nikka, waving the stone lord bartender over to refill her glass.

"I'm not naive," said Delilah. How had Iris described naive again? Someone who did things for others without caring what people thought? If that was the case, Delilah was certainly not naive.

Nikka watched her flute fill up with expensive bubbly, not even deigning to respond to Delilah until she'd had a sip. "Iris. Hmm. Let me guess… she has one of the sights?"

"The other kind of Iris," said Delilah, the whiskey beginning to hit her. "Green witch."

"Oof, way worse. She'll definitely be put on an ice floe. Not that I've ever heard of a green witch living in the city anyway, at least not for long."

"I don't feel like talking about this," said Delilah. "No offense."

"Oh yes, you're not naive at all," Nikka taunted. "As long as you don't talk about something, it doesn't exist."

"Fine then, I'm naive. Now if you don't mind, I'm just gonna sit here with my Manhattan," said Delilah.

Nikka flagged down the bartender again and asked him to fill another flute. "I'm sorry, darling. I didn't mean to get under your skin. Here, please have some. It's Dom '90, probably older than you are."

Not wanting to make a scene, Delilah accepted the drink and took a sip. It was in fact very, very good.

"I'll say one more thing and then leave you alone," started Nikka. "It's probably for the best. Between you and your Iris, that is. I'm sure she's perfectly lovely but… there's no measuring up to a death witch. Sure, people might hate you and call you names and do this, that, and the other, but it's because they know, deep inside, they can never measure up. You're just saving yourself a heartbreak, dear."

~IRIS~

As a child, Nanna Anna would take Iris to Times Square every weekend. That is, before Iris's migraines and dizzy spells started. But once they'd gotten so bad that Iris couldn't even get on the subway without feeling sick, Nanna Anna halted their routine, promising they'd go again when Iris was better. But by the time Iris understood what was happening to her and how she might mitigate or at least tolerate the effects of being in large crowds, it was Nanna Anna who was sick. By then, Iris was almost done with high school and even though she'd promised Nanna every weekend they would "see Times Square" by watching clips of it online, excuses came up over and over.

Before long, Nanna Anna was gone.

Iris marched her way out of the Times Square Station, taking deep breaths and holding onto the one thing that had ever made it easier for her to tolerate huge crowds–rage. It was an emotion she loathed and one she refused to cultivate within her but today all bets were off. Iris shoved her way past lollygagging tourists and obnoxious street performers and went to where she and Nanna used to stand, right under the jumbotrons where 7th Avenue and Broadway crossed.

X marks the spot, that's what Nanna would say, thought Iris, still fuming from the loss of the garden.

She was steady, for a few minutes. But as the crowd changed over with the rush of pedestrians going and coming from every direction, Iris began to feel her legs get weak.

I can do this.

Iris leaned against the wall under the bright, flickering jumbotrons. Her pulse was erratic and a cold sweat ran down her back.

I can do this!

She slid down the wall and onto the twin ends of a copper standpipe, using it as a seat. As her head lolled forward, passersby looked at her warily, some of them moving out of their way to avoid her. Her head throbbed and her hands and feet felt swollen. The constant yammering of the crowd mixed with the blaring advertisements and side street traffic noise, the sound feeling to Iris like the rising wall of a tsunami. She clutched her face and pressed her fingers against her cheek like she might burst through the skin and bone to relieve the building sinus pressure. She tried to swallow, but couldn't, and the more she focused on it the more anxious and panicked she became.

I can...

Something very strange happened next. The world appeared to bend in half, the filthy sidewalk street swinging up at Iris like a snapped mousetrap and the concrete smacking her in the face. Stranger still was how everyone around her was able to keep walking, just at a tilted angle, and it wasn't until she saw her smoke-stained bucket hat lying a few feet away did Iris realize she had fallen over.

Some in the crowd stopped to stare and snap pictures and videos of Iris, the bright camera lights of their phones blinding her. She tried to look away but her body refused to do anything but shake uncontrollably.

The last thing she remembered before she lost consciousness was cursing New York City with every fiber of her failure of a body.

Two Broken Witches

~IRIS~

Iris was lucky. Had there not been a blood witch with the EMTs who picked her up, she would've spent who knows how many nights in a city hospital with a huge bill to show for it. Instead, the blood witch was able to diagnose Iris on the spot, allowing her and the other EMTs to take her to a quiet clinic on the west side so she could recuperate. Still, by the time she was able to walk around again, it was almost midnight. She took a taxi home, relieved to find her apartment building still standing but far less relieved to see Delilah sitting on its stoop, looking distraught.

"Where the fuck have you been," scowled Delilah. She was about to go on but then eyed the apartment building windows suspiciously, grabbing Iris brusquely by the arm and practically shoving her back into their apartment.

"Answers. Now." Not only was Delilah pissed, but she also looked halfway between drunk and hungover.

"There was a fire in the lot. I lost my phone getting away," explained Iris.

"Yes, I know there was a fire. I've been sitting outside for six goddamn hours smelling smoke and wondering if you were dead. *How* in the fucking world was there a fire? And where were you?" Delilah asked.

"I don't know," said Iris, still not ready to give Marco up.

It wasn't that she felt anywhere close to bad for him–certainly not after this morning–but between the fire and seeing the state Delilah was in, Iris didn't trust the death witch not to knock his door down and kill him where he stood. Could she even do that? Iris didn't know, but she didn't want to find out. She continued:

"I was out planting seedlings and some of the dry weeds

must have caught fire. Maybe someone threw a cigarette out or something…"

Delilah wasn't buying it. "A day after you start working on it? Pretty fucking coincidental."

Iris's rage over the lost seedlings and the garden lot sat in her belly like a glowing hot coal.

"Why are you treating me like an arson suspect?" snapped Iris. "And forget about me, where were *you*? We got that lawsuit email this morning and you didn't even text me!"

"You didn't text me either!" shouted Delilah.

"Why is it that I'm always chasing you and you're always running away? At the bar that night, when I grew the vines in your room, in the shower, when I offered to see you at work, you're always saying no or later or some other *bullshit* excuse."

Delilah seethed, her shoulders heaving. "I fucked up the paperwork, okay?" she spat out. "That's why I didn't want to talk. The guy who was supposed to approve it was one of the workers you had your thing with in Central Park–"

"*My* thing?"

"You know what I mean. His boss was the old guy and he said he wouldn't help, alright? So that is fucked. But you know what, the plan was fucked anyway. How the hell is a stupid garden supposed to convince these people not to sue us, let alone keep Alan's kids from selling the building?"

"For the last time, it's Arthur! Arthur was our landlord, Arthur Kowalczyk. And good to know you thought my idea was stupid. I'm glad you let me go along with it like an idiot," said Iris. She paced back and forth. "When were you going to tell me that, huh? After I raised all the seedlings? After I made a dozen videos about it? After we're, like, bankrupt or whatever from the lawsuit?"

"Hate to break it to you, but those videos aren't doing anything," Delilah said, voice dripping acid. "Unless your goal was to get some of the nastiest comments I've ever read. And just so you know–" Delilah held her tongue.

"What is it?" pushed Iris.

"Nothing," said Delilah.

"Oh I get it, the big bad death witch is too afraid to say what she's thinking to the idiot flower girl. So brave."

Delilah clenched her fists and made a snarling face. "Forget the lawsuit, okay? And finding a place. I'm gonna have enough money soon for us not to have to worry about gardens or social media or any of this crap."

That caught Iris off guard. There was only one way Delilah could have that much money. "Tell me you didn't…"

"Look, your heart was in the right place but we need to be real. A garden's not going to solve this, money is."

"I can't believe you," said Iris, seeing red. "You took a death witch job? For who? Wall Street? The Department of Defense? The NYPD? Come on, tell me who you whored yourself out to."

"If you were anyone else, I'd…" started Delilah, her jaw clenched.

"You'd what?" Iris asked.

"It's for people trying to keep Keller from getting elected, okay?"

"So *now* you care who's mayor. What happened to 'they'll just make us get ID cards' or whatever? Guess you'll care for the right price after all. But you're a death witch, so go figure."

Somewhere, under all her rage and exhaustion and pain over that morning's loss, Iris knew she had gone too far. Delilah looked away with an odd, broken smile on her face. She shook her head.

"You still didn't tell me where you were," she said quietly.

"I lost my phone in the fire. Then I…" Iris sighed. "I went to Times Square. And I collapsed."

"What the fuck were you doing in Times Square?" asked Delilah. "You couldn't handle a crowded bar the other night with your condition. Are you trying to kill yourself?"

"In between all your whining and crying about being a death witch, do you *ever* stop to think what it might be like to not be able to go into a crowded bar? Or a packed subway? Or one of the most popular tourist spots in the city?"

Delilah said nothing.

"Of course not. Because–" She felt a surge of renewed anger and regretted what she said next before the words were even out of her mouth. "–because even when they're not being shills for sale, death witches are always, always looking out for themselves."

"That's not fair," said Delilah.

"No, it isn't." Iris stared down Delilah's blue-eyed gaze,

determined not to break even if it meant her eyeballs fell out of her head. "I went to Times Square to conquer my 'condition' and I failed, proving everyone right about what they keep saying: green witches don't belong in New York. So I'm leaving."

Iris hadn't expected to say that last part but it just came out and, when it did, the words set quickly like wet cement.

Delilah sneered. "Whoa, who's the big bad brave girl now?" she asked. "Guess when the going gets tough, Iris Williams gets on a train and skips town. At least you won't need my dirty death witch money to relocate to some backwoods outside of Utica or wherever you wind up. You're a coward, you know that?"

"The going gets tough?" repeated a flabbergasted Iris. "The going got tough for me twenty years ago! Get the fuck over yourself! And if you want to see a coward..." Iris was now the one who held her tongue.

"If I want to see a coward, then what?" challenged Delilah.

Don't say it, a voice inside Iris said. *Don't go there.*

But she was too angry and tired to listen.

"I was going to say 'If you want to see a coward, look in the mirror' but I don't think you have the guts to do that."

Delilah looked off to the side, glaring at a spot on the wall for what felt like minutes. "You know what? I don't need this shithole anymore, I have a real job. So whether you go to bumblefuck nowhere or stay here, I give a flying fuck. I'm sorry I was such a burden on your pretty little green witch life, but don't worry, I'm sure we won't see each other again."

The death watch stomped her way to the door and then stopped. She turned around. Then she marched to the coffee table and snatched up the calla lily she had given Iris, leaving without another word.

And then Iris was all alone, like she always knew she would be.

~DELILAH~

"Way to go, death bitch," Delilah said to herself as she stormed out of the apartment building. "Way to go."

MEETING EXPECTATIONS

~DELILAH~

Seven nights at the Baccarat Hotel in midtown was nearly ten grand, just all that less than what Delilah had spent on rent in the past year. Her room, like the hotel itself, was cast in pristine white with black metal and dark wood accents, creating a feeling of sterile luxury, as if no outside air or dirt had ever made its way into the Baccarat. An army of indistinguishable staff busied themselves constantly with mundane tasks to keep up the hotel's appearance, like dusting tables or fluffing chair pillows, scurrying off every time Delilah or any other guest wanted to use whichever hotel nook they were tending to. Never before had Delilah been treated with such privilege. Even down at the hotel bar, which had a waiting list every single night, there was a seat reserved for her after the maître d' took notice of her.

Delilah called in sick from her shifts at McManus and Style Revival instead of quitting, not wanting a blowout over the phone to ruin her first week at the Baccarat. Rather than go back to the apartment to pick up clothing, she bought herself an all-new wardrobe and with her newly found free time, she did something she'd never done before–she worked on her death magick.

In a midday tipsy stupor, Delilah came up with her initial plan to pick up bugs from a pet store, figuring that not only were the insects probably going to be fed to reptiles anyway but that she'd also already exterminated a metric shitton of lanternflies. What harm would a few more creepy crawlies do? But by the time she found a pet store near the hotel, she was sobering up and couldn't bring herself to go through with it. Delilah settled for going to a supermarket and buying cuts of meat to work on her decomposition skills.

It was an unglamorous scene for the glamorous hotel bathroom, with Delilah working on poultry and seafood to speed up and slow down the rates of decay. For the first hour, Delilah was fighting nausea after each act of magick, but the drills soon paid off, making it easier and easier for the death witch to throttle her ability. Decay wasn't all that different from exterminating, she realized; if exterminating was a wild punch thrown with all her weight, decay was a slow, focused jab, the basic motion the same and all the difference in intensity and speed.

As she neared the end of her stack of chicken breasts, Delilah decided she would experiment. Instead of a "slow, focused jab", she wanted to see what would happen if she tried the opposite, like pulling back a punch that never came. She closed her eyes and concentrated, withdrawing the focus of her death magick from the poultry more, and more, and more…

Bwak Bwak Bwa-bwaaaak!

Delilah fell backwards at the loud clucking sound in her ears.

What the fuck was that? she wondered, her head spinning as she stared at the bright bathroom lights.

She resisted looking at the chicken breast on the tile floor, heart racing at the thought of what she might see there. Sucking a breath in through her teeth, Delilah whipped her head towards it. The chicken breast was still there, looking exactly as it had before.

"Great, now I'm hearing things," she said to herself as she sat up, trying to laugh away the episode.

But Delilah didn't try the experiment again, content to decay through the rest of the meat and forget about mystery chickens squawking in her ears.

Aside from practice, Delilah mostly drank. It was too much, even for her, but there was no one to judge her for her hangovers or worry that she was overdoing it. One time she got so drunk she turned up the lights in her room and took off her clothes, taking videos of herself walking around naked. The idea was that she would rewatch them in the morning to prove Iris wrong, that she wasn't a coward, though when morning came, Delilah deleted them in a bleary-eyed haze.

She tried so hard not to think of Iris. The easiest way was to imagine that Iris really had left New York and was surrounded by trees and plants and all that other shit somewhere upstate, leaving Delilah to waste her days away however she wanted. Even then, Delilah couldn't resist the temptation to check for new videos on the Two_Broke_Witches accounts, doing rounds through TikTok, YouTube, and Instagram and only finding nasty new comments. She eventually got so sick of them she made her own new accounts as "DevilDeathB" to attack back, laying into every mean comment she could find until her temper was wound tight.

Delilah barely slept and barely ate, each day a little fuzzier than the last. She stopped checking her email and all news and social media except for the comments on the Two_Broke_Witches accounts. And the only texts she didn't dismiss were the ones from the Invisible Man, Ralph Ellison.

He came by twice to see her. The first time was with a brick of hundred-dollar bills, enough to cover Delilah's hotel stay for the next month and then some; he told her it would be the first of many. The second was to assign Delilah a job.

"We're going to start small," he told her while sitting in her disheveled hotel room, Delilah refusing maid service for a week straight now. "Just to ease you in."

"Sure. Whatever." Delilah was irritable from her latest hangover.

Ralph gave one of his unnerving flat-lipped lizard smiles. "You know about the fire that was behind your apartment building, I presume?"

"You mean in the community lot?" asked Delilah, knowing there was something off about Iris's story. Her stomach churned.

"That's the one alright. So you know it was no accident?"

Delilah reached up and pulled at the piercings in her ears until it hurt.

"You didn't know..." said a placidly amused Ralph. "Interesting. Yes, we believe it was one of your neighbors. Marco Galeano."

"He doesn't happen to be thin, average height, and a little on the older side by any chance?" she asked, beginning to feel very warm.

"Yes, he fits that description. He's in apartment 4E. Lives alone. He's been there for decades."

"He set a fire and he hasn't even been arrested?" Delilah's blood thumped in her ears.

Ralph tapped his pointer finger slowly against his leg and said, "There doesn't appear to be an investigation in progress. The FDNY deemed the fire… accidental, it seems."

"What exactly is it that you want from me?" asked Delilah.

"As far as we can tell, Marco Galeano spends an inordinate amount of time hating paras, online and off, as well as spreading pro-Keller memes and disinformation. In the grand scheme of things he is not material–he is no mastermind, just another relay point making the world a colder one for people like us. But we thought that you deserved a chance to set things right with him."

"Set things right… what's that supposed to mean?"

Ralph got up. "You're a death witch, Ms. Cruz. You know what it means. Message me when it's done."

She walked him to the hotel room's door and watched as he meandered down the hallway and then disappeared from sight.

~IRIS~

I failed, proving everyone right about what they keep saying: green witches don't belong in New York. So I'm leaving.

It had been an anger-fueled touch of spite to end Iris's rant, but as soon as she said those words–"So I'm leaving"–Iris realized it was true. Her parents had rejected her. New York had rejected her. Delilah had rejected her. She had nothing left in the city anymore.

But she couldn't just storm off like Delilah. She had to figure out where she would go and what she would do with her plants, along with all the other loose ends she had to tie up before she left New York for good. Without a phone, Iris was forced to coordinate everything on her aging, wheezy laptop, starting with the easiest chore–quitting the Strand. All that took was an email and an apology, and Iris figured she'd be replaced by the end of the week.

Deciding where to go was harder and Iris had to wait until the next day to even wrap her head around that task, suffering through a bitter, sleepless night spent sobbing until her eyes were sore and her stomach hurt. Her mood spread to every plant in her room, the ferns and succulents and flowers and vines retreating into themselves like a winter frost had just descended.

It took Iris a mind-numbing day of research using some of Coven Hub's outdated green witch guides to pick a course of action. Eventually, she would need to figure out something more permanent, but take a baby step first–a night or two of camping in a bread-and-breakfast town so that she could retreat to creature comforts should she need them while acclimating to… well, what exactly? Having only lived in NYC, she wasn't totally sure. But she thought that the green witch in her would come out even more strongly once she was somewhere more verdant than the city and lead her to a place and a lifestyle where she could finally thrive rather than simply try to survive.

Iris settled on Cold Spring, which was a little more than an hour from the city but looked like it could've been several states away. Perfect. That left the question of what to do with Maddy, Philly, Carl, and the rest of her plants. She couldn't take them all with her, she knew that, but she also couldn't just abandon them. As Iris stared out through her bedroom window at the garden lot that was still caution taped off, she decided she would relocate her plants there, hiding them among the remaining weeds and replanting them in what fresh soil was left so that whatever happened, they would have the best chance of a happy life. Even if that was without her.

She wouldn't do that during the day though, not when Marco or anyone else might see her. So Iris waited until the dead of night and moved the plants out in shifts, wearing one of the black hoodies Delilah had left behind to keep as low a profile as possible; it stung Iris how much it smelled of the death witch. One corner of the lot had escaped the fire and that's where Iris spent her time, digging the dirt out with her bare hands so that she could be sure she was leaving each and every one of her plants with the best spot possible to keep growing.

It was hours of planting before Iris was ready to search for any seedlings that had survived the fire and, as the lack of plant auras already told her, there were none. Dozens and dozens of seedlings had been lost.

While Iris worked, she thought constantly about Delilah. In all honesty, Delilah was right–the garden *was* a stupid idea, another one of Iris's idiotic hopeful gambits that she prayed would work.

So was the social media campaign which, unlike Delilah, Iris hadn't monitored at all, having no idea what people were saying. When she saw the vitriol though, it only underscored how right Delilah was and how dumb Iris had been for thinking such a plan would work. But that was Iris, wasn't it? Dumb, hopeful, and hopeless.

Only one thing still stuck in Iris like a thorn: calling Delilah a coward for not wanting to look in the mirror. That was low. For all of Delilah's frustrating worry about her body, she had only been caring and supportive when it came to Iris's body and–most importantly–Iris's real hair. Maybe the most ironic part was that Iris didn't even stand behind her words–she adored the way Delilah looked and didn't care what anyone else thought. To Iris, Delilah was a wondrous, rare flower, something not for everyone perhaps but exhibiting a beauty and power and surprising depth that that Iris had been–

Don't say it.

–falling in love with.

Iris spent the next two days eyeing the singed garden lot to make sure Marco or anyone else wasn't abusing her plants, picking up some cheap camping gear at the Salvation Army, and finalizing her exit from the Strand. After she'd gathered what she needed for her trip to Cold Spring, she only had another bit of unfinished business: the vines in her and Delilah's bedroom.

She wanted to move them into the community garden, but from the moment her fingers tried to peel them off the walls, she knew they would let themselves be torn apart rather than budge. Even though they constantly whined about wanting more sun and soil and room to sprawl, they refused to leave the space where they and Iris had spent so many nights next to each other. It crushed her to think that the same vines that had often been so cagey and quiet now didn't want to leave the cramped apartment coated with Iris's presence.

"You can't come with me," said Iris, tearing up as she ran her hand across the vine leaves. "Please, let me put you somewhere else. I don't belong here, but you…"

The vine leaves fluttered against her hand in protest.

"I can't," said Iris, tears running down. "Anywhere you want, I'll figure it out. I just… I need to…"

As if intuiting Iris's deepest thoughts, the vines stopped their fluttering anguish. They stilled for a minute and then in a bizarre motion Iris thought plants incapable of, a cluster of the vine leaves turned in on itself, working their spade leaves against one winding stem to break off a small leaf cutting that tumbled to the bedroom floor.

Iris picked it up and held it gingerly in her palm. Then she filled up every last glass, bowl, and pitcher they had with water and put them under the vines in her and Delilah's room so they would be okay as long as possible. With a roller bag full of clothes and other essentials, she left her room, feeling the vine leaves looking at her before she closed the door.

She had one last thing to do and that was a handwritten note to Marco. Knowing his first name, it wasn't hard to find what unit he was in; she left a note which would hopefully keep him from harming her plants:

You know who this is. I don't know why you did what you did and I don't care. Just leave my plants alone, please. They didn't do anything to you and we'll be gone soon. You win. All I care about now is leaving this place better than I found it.

And that was Iris's last act as a tenant of Unit 1B in the building on Madison Street.

The Threshold

~IRIS~

Five days. That's all it took Iris to wrap up twenty-six years of life in New York City.

The train to Cold Spring was empty, leaving Iris alone as they pulled out of Grand Central to stare out the window at endless green on her way to the Hudson Valley. When she arrived, Iris wandered around the quaint tourist town, amazed at how much easier she could breathe. There were antique shops and craft stores and diners, and she caught herself laughing at how much Delilah would hate it here before remembering Iris would never have the chance to witness it.

Iris stashed her luggage in a train locker at the station, only taking with her a camping pack and the vine clipping, who she'd started calling Vin, for company. It was over a hamburger and fries that the reality of what Iris was about to do set in. There would be no heat, no bathroom, and no food except what she brought with her into the woods, which was just a box of protein bars for now. And although keeping close to plant life would help Iris sustain herself, she didn't know if there were limits to how long she would be able to go without a proper meal.

But she wasn't going deep into the woods, having planned a route that would take her no farther than an hour off the main hiking trail; if she needed to eat real food, she could just come back to town. What upset Iris more were the things she hadn't considered: no bedtime routine with her plants, no makeup, no city sounds. It was enough to make her homesick. But there was no turning back now. NYC was in the past, a place that for Iris only held a pending lawsuit and twelve days left in a crummy apartment.

And your vines. And Philly and Carl and Maddy and–

Iris silenced the voice in her head, wolfed down the rest of the burger, and trekked out into the woods.

There were a handful of other people hiking the trails outside of Cold Spring, but none of them seemed particularly interested in talking to a dark-skinned green witch with a long pink wig. That made it easy for Iris to slip off the trail and into the woods, using a paper map that itched her fingers and markers on the trees to navigate without a phone–not that she would've gotten service in the woods anyway. It surprised her how the trees became so dense so quickly, but what was even more surprising was how quiet they were. If this were the city, the trees would've been incessantly chatty–especially this many of them so close together–but Iris barely heard a peep from them, their auras dimmed and disinterested in her.

Or were they being dismissive? She'd encountered a few uppity plants here or there, but an entire forest? It was unthinkable.

Once Iris reached Marker 4801, she dropped her pack and set up camp. She'd chosen this spot on the train ride up, based on some rough guesses about elevation and possible rainfall, but honestly she'd been expecting the woods to tell her if it was a good spot once she'd arrived. But the arboreal silence persisted and Iris was left to trust her rudimentary map reading skills and hoped the trees would warm to her.

Iris woke to Vin scratching at her cheek. He'd grown nearly a half a foot from his paper cup planter and as Iris stared bewildered at him inside the Salvation Army A-frame tent, a panic washed over her.

She didn't remember setting up camp.

She remembered arriving and double checking her map but after that, there was nothing but a blank spot in her memories. It was dark outside the tent and Iris struggled to remember when finished her burger and took off for the trail. Early afternoon? A little later? That meant it had to be five or six hours later, maybe more. Maybe much more.

Iris swung her flashlight around, looking for Marker 4801. She found it, but it was almost a hundred feet away when Iris had been sure she'd dropped her pack right under the marker. She closed her eyes and listened for the trees, trying to hear them.

Talk to me, she thought as loudly as she could. *I'm a green witch. I can understand, not like those other people.*

Silence.

Iris went back inside her tent and grabbed Vin, holding him by her side as she closed her eyes again.

See? This little one trusts me. You can trust me too, I promise.

There was a loud, angry crash of leaves, like a boulder had just barreled through the woods, the force of it enough to ruffle Iris's clothes and nearly blow her wig off. She looked around, swinging the flashlight in long sweeping arcs. Her tent was gone. Vin scratched wildly at Iris's hand.

"They're just afraid," she said to Vin, her own heart racing. "They don't–"

And then she heard the trees loud and clear, dozens or perhaps hundreds of them talking to her all at once in one big booming voice:

OUTSIDER. YOU DO NOT BELONG HERE.

Iris was shaking, having never heard any flora shout at her like that. She reached up with trepidation to pull off her wig, revealing the satiny pink petal hair underneath in hopes that it would prove who she was to the forest. The hostile air of the deep wood remained unchanged.

"We can just go," said Iris, now sure there was no way she was going to win over these trees. "If you just let me see the markers, I can get back on my own…"

Then there was a peculiar sound. It was like scratching on wood mixed with the sound of movement underground. Iris's body understood it before her mind did, a pang in her stomach so heavy it made her sick.

The forest was laughing at her.

And then it went deathly silent. There was no more laughing or shouting or movement, the entire woods of Cold Spring not making a single plant or animal sound. Iris swung the flashlight again, searching for Marker 4801, but it was gone.

~DELILAH~

Delilah had never killed anyone. But when she was sixteen, she had come very close. There was no drama to it and no intention behind it, just an angry sixteen-year-old Delilah who had been so humiliated by another sixteen-year-old girl that she snapped. The girl, Mary, was a prom queen type who Delilah had been crushing on throughout all of high school. And Mary had drawn a picture. That was it. It was an exaggerated caricature of Delilah, with a long, pointed chin, huge ears, and a nose like a bird's beak, her head attached to a cutout of some greased-up bodybuilder. It was supposed to be a joke between Mary and one of her cool kid friends, but when a teacher saw it being passed around and demanded to know who made it, it spread like wildfire.

That was twelve years ago and the last Delilah checked, Mary was still in a coma from what Delilah had done to her.

Getting to Marco would be easy. The only hurdle would be his apartment door, which Delilah couldn't very well knock down without causing a scene. But she knew that Unit 4E faced the alleyway and that unlike most apartment lines, it had its own fire escape. All Delilah had to do was wait for Marco to leave with his windows wide open and then she could waltz in and wait for him to return.

To achieve that, Delilah would have to take a page from Marco's book.

The evening after Ralph Ellison had come to see her for the second time, Delilah returned to her building, dressed in sweats, a baggy sweater, and a new baseball cap with her knockoff Ray-Bans. She walked up to the fourth floor, hoping she wouldn't run into any other neighbors. This was the riskiest part of the plan–if any of the neighbors saw and recognized her, she'd have to scrap everything and start from scratch. She reached Marco Galeano's apartment and pressed her ear to the door, hearing TV sounds. It was time to get started.

She took out what was left of her patchouli fragrance and dumped the entire bottle along the base of the apartment door. Then she took out a plastic baggie of diced salmon, sprinkling the fish on top of the heady cologne and concentrating as she decayed the fish rapidly, the funk awful and pungent almost immediately.

Making as little noise as she could, Delilah hurried back down the stairs and out the building to go wait in its alleyway, her eyes fixed on the fourth-floor fire escape.

It took fifteen minutes, but sure enough Marco soon opened his fire escape window all the way to air his apartment out, making a retching sound as he did. By now he'd discovered the rotten fish for sure and–since the building didn't have trash chutes–Marco would have to take the mess down himself, giving Delilah time to get into his apartment. Thanks to her height, it was easy to clamber up the fire escape's hanging ladder and to climb the fire escape on the side railings rather than risk being spotted on each landing's metal stairs.

When Delilah reached Marco's window, she waited, listening to the still-blaring TV before slowly peeking inside. As far as she could tell, the apartment was empty.

Here we go, she thought.

Delilah crept into the apartment. It was old–even older than hers–and there were stacks of newspapers and magazines everywhere. The walls were painted a hideous 80s shade of yellow and a high-pile brown carpet seemed to cover every inch of the apartment's floor. On the TV was *Wheel of Fortune,* though the picture was fuzzy with a permanent glitch line on one side of the screen. Delilah could smell the stink of the rotten fish and patchouli in the air and tried to not gag as she looked for a good ambush spot, settling on the hallway to the sad-looking single bedroom.

She waited.

The door opened and then slammed shut. There was a loud groaning sigh.

"Friggin disgusting," said Marco, sounding nearly as drunk as he did when he barged into Delilah and Iris's apartment. As he walked back to his beat-up couch that had last seen better days twenty ago, she came at him from behind, shoving him hard to the ground.

He turned over with a terrified look in his eyes. He was much older than she would've guessed under his ski mask and thinner too, like he was wasting away to nothing.

You won't have to waste away much longer, she thought. With a grotesque matter-of-factness, she realized that when she was done, she could probably decay him too and leave little evidence she was ever there. Somewhere inside of her, an Iris-tinged part of Delilah rebelled at the idea.

"Y-you!" he cried. "I thought you were gone!"

Delilah held her hand out to him and he flinched.

"Keep your voice down," she warned him. "Or else."

He cowered against the side of the couch.

Now was Delilah's chance. All she had to do was give one wild, unfettered thrust with her magick and Marco Galeano would go straight past coma to join the rest of the dead. She hesitated.

"Why did you set that fire?" she asked.

Marco was full body trembling and Delilah could see that he'd peed himself.

"I told her she shouldn't have been there," he mewled. "I wasn't trying to hurt her, I just… I… you were never supposed to be in this building. It was not for you or her…"

"Her who? Iris?"

Marco nodded weakly.

"You talked to her?" asked Delilah, confused.

"I… I saw her there, in the old lot, maybe a week and a half ago," said Marco. "I told her New York wasn't going to be safe for her, not after the election. I told her how to call the sanitation department to get all that junk removed. I swear, I didn't know she'd be there when I… when I…"

She didn't tell me any of this, thought Delilah. *Why?*

"You think that excuses anything?" she asked. "You think that lets you just burn down a garden and put our lives at risk? We sleep fifty feet away from there!"

You don't sleep there anymore, a voice in Delilah's head reminded her.

"It wasn't supposed to get that big!" Marco said in a whisper-shout, barely able to control his blubbering. "It was just supposed to scare you, that's it. I swear to God! I won't touch the plants either, I promise!"

"What plants…?"

For the first time since Delilah had ambushed him, hope shone through Marco's terror. He went to stand and Delilah shoved her open palm in his face.

"On the kitchen table," he said. "There's a note…"

Keeping her hand stretched towards Marco the entire time, Delilah shuffled over to the kitchen table. There was a mound of unopened envelopes and half-finished crosswords and yellowed New York Times Sunday magazines; on top of the mound was a letter in familiar handwriting. Iris.

Delilah quickly scanned the note.

She also knew he set the fire. I don't get it, why didn't she–

And then it clicked. Iris didn't tell Delilah for the same reason Delilah was standing in Marco Galeano's apartment right now, because Iris was afraid Delilah would kill him. A flash of anger tunneled her vision as she bristled with Iris's unspoken judgment of her, but that flash faded as she realized something else, something that had been staring her in the face for years and years.

It was up to her who she was going to be.

If Delilah always saw herself as a death witch holding back her killing nature, that's all she'd ever be, a bomb waiting to go off. It wasn't about whether or not she acted like a death witch "should", it was about deciding to be different, inside and out. Iris understood that about Delilah when Delilah herself was too busy feeling shitty and ugly and broken to let herself grow into the best, truest version of herself–and to realize she had met someone who already saw that version of her.

Delilah lowered her hand. "Let me ask you something," she said to Marco as she looked around his apartment, taking in the old upholstery and stacks of saved newspapers. "How long have you lived here?"

"Thirty-nine years," he said, still trying to gain her favor.

"So before it was okay to come out as a para," said Delilah. "Well, more okay, I guess. You know that friend of mine, Iris, she grew up in New York."

"I know," Marco said softly. "She told me."

Delilah hadn't expected that. "Did you know I work at a thrift shop? And that I'm a bartender?"

"Aren't you a, um…" Marco lowered his voice to an almost imperceptible whisper. "Death witch?"

"No, I'm a bartender," said Delilah, never more proud to have pulled long boring daytime shifts at McManus for the last five years. "And Iris works at a bookstore."

'Why are you telling me this?" asked Marco.

"Because I want you to know we're *normal*. As normal as anyone else in this city, anyway. We're not rich. We're not part of some elite illuminati. We're just two normal women who just so happen to be witches and who actually like–liked–living here, believe it or not. And that garden that you burned down…" She looked at Iris's letter.

All I care about now is leaving this place better than I found it.
"…I'm going to nurse it back to life."

"What are you going to do to me?" asked Marco pitifully.

"Why would I do anything to you? I'm just some bartender with an interest in gardening," said Delilah. She took Iris's letter and went to the apartment door. Just as she was about to step into the hallway, Delilah turned back to Marco.

"You lived here a long time," she said. "Have you ever thought about leaving this place better than you found it?"

~IRIS~

The forest had grown in the night. That was the only explanation for why Iris couldn't find a single tree marker or any hint of the Cold Spring hiking trails. She wandered from sunup to sundown with Vin, her only food two protein bars she'd found buried under old fallen leaves. The trees continued to stonewall her and even though Iris was surrounded by dense, lush woods, the only bit of plant life she could detect with an aura was Vin. Iris did her best to walk in the arc of the sun, sure that as long as she kept as straight as possible she had to eventually find some trail or river's edge or something else besides the endless forest. And yet, after ten hours of walking she was still surrounded by silent trees. One thought kept bubbling up in Iris's mind:

I'm never getting out of here.

It was cold at night without her camping gear, Iris packing herself under a bed of leaves in an attempt to keep warm. Still, it wasn't enough and before long she was shivering as she tried to fall asleep. What happened next felt like it was out of a fever dream, though she knew in her gut it was true–Vin was growing faster than any plant had ever grown for her, spinning himself into a thick, leafy dome of intertwined vines that created a shelter to block out the cold night air.

Iris only had one dream that night, but she had it again and again and again. In it, she had finally found her way out of the woods after descending a steep slope covered in compost and dotted with rotting tree stumps. At the bottom of the slope was the base of a stone cliff with a normal-looking door in it, just like the one to the apartment on Madison Street. A figure in a hooded black cloak was holding the door open and as soon as Iris saw the strong, long-fingered pale hand of the figure, she knew who it belonged to.

"Is this the way home?" Iris asked in her dream.

The figure shut the door and pointed back up the slope. At the very top of it, on a scarecrow of a tree, were two ravens cawing at Iris. She was afraid of them at first and then she felt like they were trying to tell her something she couldn't understand.

Iris woke in the middle of the night and when she fell asleep again, the dream started anew.

In the morning, Iris set out again, carrying the vine-basket Vin had grown into on her back. She rationed the protein bars, trying to spend as much time under the sun to refresh herself but finding few open patches in the thick foliage of the Cold Spring woods. As she did yesterday, she followed the sun, her feet beginning to blister and her body feeling heavy and weak. She spent another night with Vin shielding her and dreamed the same dream, but this time there was more.

In this version, Iris climbed her way back up the steep slope to the tree with the ravens perched on it. She felt like she was waiting for someone, but she didn't know who. Even though it was against every instinct she had, something told her to wait there in that very spot and to not move. The ravens cawed at her, getting Iris's attention, and when she leaned in close to their dead tree perch, she saw a dried bird's nest tucked into the crook of a broken branch. Inside the nest was a petrified calla lily. When Iris looked up from the nest, the ravens were gone and a swarm of lanternflies were crawling along the tree's branches, towards the bird's nest with the lily inside.

On Iris's third day trekking through the woods, she ran out of her rationed protein bars. The water she'd been sustaining herself with, foraged from dewy leaves and tiny puddles, was becoming scarcer, as if the woods themselves were drying up. Iris was running out of time.

Of all the things she could've thought about during her third endless slog through the woods, she kept coming back to one–wishing she hadn't called Delilah a coward.

I'm the coward. I ran. I could've stayed, I could've tried harder. But it was easier to run. And here I am, no better off.

Another thought crossed her mind.

I wish Delilah was here.

Iris didn't remember falling asleep that night, but just like the last two nights, she dreamt. It was again the same dream, with the trip down the slope to the base of the cliffs, then back up to the dead tree that was covered in lanternflies. This time Iris snatching the petrified calla lily out of the nest before the insects could swarm it.

Leaves crunched underfoot as someone approached from behind. It was the figure in the hooded black cloak, the ravens now perched on either of its shoulders. Looking closer, Iris realized this figure was different from the one she spoke to before.

"Who are you?" asked Iris.

The figure pulled back its hood. The ghostly face of a death witch stared back at Iris, the eyes silver and the lips unnaturally black. It reminded Iris of Delilah, if Delilah had the weight of thousands upon thousands of years on her.

"It's almost time to go," the unknown death witch said.

"Go where?" asked Iris.

"To the ground. To return to what was."

Iris wanted to wake up. She willed herself to wake up. But as hard as she tried, she could not shake herself out of the dream.

"I don't want to go," said Iris.

"Everyone goes, sooner or later," said the figure. She held out her hand for Iris to take, the nails disturbingly long.

In a daze, Iris handed the figure the petrified lily instead. The figure looked down at it curiously. She smiled to herself, the expression awkward as if she didn't quite remember what a smile was.

"Very well," the figure said. She looked to the ravens on her shoulders and they flitted over to the lanternfly-covered tree, picking off the insects and carrying them away, dropping the dead bugs in a trail that led away from the steep slope. "Go home."

The figure started down the slope while the ravens continued their work.

"Wait! How do I get home?" asked Iris.

"You know how, city witch."

Just as Iris didn't remember going to sleep, she didn't remember waking either. But there she was, sitting in the fallen leaves of the woods, huddled under Vin for warmth. A trail of tiny lavender flames led from where she sat towards the direction Iris thought she came from.

"Okay," she said, barely able to stand up. "My brain is turning to jelly. But in case I'm not crazy, I sure hope that was a friend of yours in my dream, Delilah."

Within the hour, Iris was back on the Cold Spring hiking trail. The scant hikers she saw stared goggle-eyed at her as she nearly tumbled her way back to town, the witch stopping at the first stream she found to slake her thirst. Her camping pack was gone, but she was lucky to still have her wallet and the key to the train station locker where she'd stashed her roller bag and the rest of her belongings. Taking out a change of clothes, Iris went down to the river and bathed in the frigid water. Her wig was long gone too, lost somewhere in the deep woods, and when Iris dipped her head into the river she could feel her natural hair luxuriate in the nutrient-rich freshwater.

With Vin–now a cradle of vines that had likely saved her life–across from her, Iris gorged herself on a hamburger at the same place where she'd had the one before her trek. She was so hungry she ordered a second and almost a third, only stopping when she remembered what the figure in her dream had called her.

City witch. Iris had no idea who that figure was supposed to be, but she liked the sound of that. And where did a city witch belong? In the city, of course.

GARDEN OF ARTHUR

~DELILAH~

Marco wasn't much of a gardener. Neither was Delilah. But they did their best, making up for what they lacked in horticulture skills with a willingness to get their hands dirty–literally. Though before Marco was willing to help, he needed to know they had permission to use the lot, worried that abuse of city property might put his Depart of Sanitation pension at risk.

"I've got bad news for you," said Delilah as she haphazardly picked out a bundle of seed packets from Home Depot's Garden Center, having no idea what she was looking for. "Once they saw I was a death witch, they blocked my application."

"I thought you were a bartender," said Marco dryly, his terror having worn off.

Delilah couldn't believe it, but the same man who had busted into her apartment and torched Iris's gardening work was actually beginning to grow on her. A little, anyway.

"Funny how people can label you like that," Delilah shot back as she tried to decide between two seed packet mixes, eventually just taking both. She was shopping with the Invisible Man's money and tried not to think about what would happen when he asked her for an update on Marco. Somehow she didn't think taking him seed shopping was what Ralph Ellison had in mind.

I'll figure something out, she thought.

"So the lot isn't approved for work?" asked Marco. "Are you sure?"

"I threatened the guy who was doing the approving, so I'm pretty damn sure," said Delilah. "Oh and I called the guy who worked for him a pussy so, yeah."

Marco took out his phone, the font large and screen painfully bright. He navigated to some ancient-looking city website and slowly tapped out the address of the lot.

Delilah scoffed. "Don't waste your time. I get it if you don't wanna work on the lot. If you still wanna help, maybe instead you can just move some stuff to the sidewalk or–"

"It's been approved," Marco said.

"Bullshit. You got the address wrong. Or the date. Or *something*."

"Nope, the approval record is right here. It was approved five days ago."

"Impossible..." Delilah set her basket of seeds down and dug her phone out of her back pocket. Between job offers, mailing list spam, and random inbox junk, she had hundreds of unread emails. She searched for "GreenThumb" and couldn't believe her eyes when she saw an email titled: *Application Approval Notice*. "But how?"

Stranger still was that another email had arrived in Delilah's inbox at the exact same time, this one without a subject line and from a personal gmail account belonging to someone named Jerome Campbell:

Ms. Cruz–I was shocked to learn that the very same community garden lot you applied for just so happened to suffer a fire the very same day you and I met. After reading the examiner's report, I was also shocked to find that not only had this lot been cleared of junk the day before our meeting, but that the only remains found after the fire appeared to be a mobile phone and a surprising number of burnt seedlings, as if someone had already been attempting to start a garden on it.

There are a lot of things wrong with this city. But I don't believe too many gardens and green spaces are among them. New York would be a far, far better place if the worst thing people did was try to make their communities nicer by planting flowers and bushes. Good luck with the garden.

"Everything okay?" asked Marco.

Delilah wiped a tear from her eye. "Uh, yeah. You're right, the application was approved. Let's get a few more seed packets and then see if we can stop by GreenThumb to pick up some tools."

"Nah, no need. Arthur kept a bunch of that stuff in the basement of the building. I have a spare key we can use to get down there."

An idea took root in Delilah's mind.

"Did you know Arthur well?" she asked Marco.

"Oh, sure. Helped him get through all the city red tape for that building. He'd pay me back in beers at this crappy little dive on the corner, 'til it got sold."

"Anyway Bar?" asked Delilah.

Marco laughed. "That's the one. Guess it's more your scene than mine these days, huh?"

"I don't know about that," Delilah said.

"If you say so…"

"Do you know Arthur's kids?"

"Jake and Andi? Sure, of course," said Marco. "Nice kids, but I doubt they know anything about managing a building. No wonder they're selling. Why do you ask?"

"No reason," said Delilah, the idea in her mind beginning to bloom.

They worked on the garden for the next two days, Delilah keeping an eye on her phone for messages from Ralph–or anyone else. Her apartment felt empty without Iris in it, but at least the vines were still there, even if Delilah couldn't imagine why Iris would leave those behind and little else. Delilah had taken to staying in Iris's room and started every morning by spritzing down the vines, hoping she wasn't overwatering them.

During the first morning, Delilah had gone to the Baccarat Hotel to checkout and pick up her belongings. Everything was how she had left it except for one thing: the calla lily she had gotten Iris had died. It looked dried out and desiccated, but Delilah wanted to take it back with her anyway. The moment she touched it, it crumbled. Had all that decay practice on the poultry and fish affected the lily too?

When Delilah went to meet Marco for their next gardening session, she saw that he wasn't alone.

More than fifteen neighbors from the building had joined him, dressed in sun hats and mud boots and overalls, the crew already hard at work tilling the torched soil and laying down fresh mulch.

"What's this?" Delilah asked him, having to step over packs of flagstone tiles someone had brought to use to build out a pathway.

"Just some concerned tenants," said Marco. He was on his knees in the fresh dirt, making small holes in the earth to drop seeds into. "Your idea to leave this place better than we found it before we all leave was pretty popular I gotta say."

"It wasn't my idea," said Delilah. "It was–"

Delilah saw her approaching the garden with shuffling steps, her cheeks gaunt and her shoulders sagging. Iris. She was dragging a roller bag behind her with some kind of basket over her shoulder that looked like it was made out of vines. Her wig was gone, her natural petaled hair underneath pushed back against her scalp. There was something different in her eyes, some kind of tenacity that hadn't been there before. Seeing Delilah, Iris picked up her shuffling pace as if the ground under her might give out at any moment.

A few of the volunteers stopped what they were doing to stare dumbly at the green witch, their eyes flicking up to the silky pink petals against Iris's scalp. When Marco saw them with their mouths hanging open, he said: "Alright everyone, there's plenty of work left and only so many hours in the day. If you've got spare hands come tell me so I can give them something to do."

The volunteers went back to their duties and Marco nodded a greeting at Iris with a small, ashamed smile before going back to seed planting. Delilah met Iris at the edge of the garden, her feet planted on the fresh soil while Iris stood on the sidewalk.

"What's going on?" Iris asked in a dazed voice.

"What happened to you?" asked Delilah almost at the same time as Iris.

Iris swept a hand across her petaled hair. "Do you like it?" she asked with a tired smile.

"I always did," said Delilah.

A bus rumbled by on the street, its brakes squealing as the driver took a sharp turn. The witches stared at each other, frozen in place.

"I–"

"You–"

They both went silent and moments later tried again.

"When–"

"If–"

Delilah's laugh nearly turned into a sob, the witch just managing to hold onto her tears.

"I was an idiot," she said. "I spent an entire year living next to this cheerful, kind, fucking *hot* green witch and I ignored her the whole time, like she was part of the wallpaper. Not that our apartment's nice enough to have wallpaper–we're lucky we have walls, honestly."

Iris gave a tiny laugh.

"And somehow, despite all my moping and brooding, I get to know this green witch," continued Delilah. "And what do you know? She's amazing. Thoughtful, courageous, sexy… and so wonderfully naive."

There were tears in both witches' eyes; Delilah felt hers start to run down her cheeks.

"But despite how amazing she is–and how much she seems into me–I can't get over my own shit. And instead of listening to her and letting her into my heart, I keep slamming the door in her face again and again. Can you imagine that? You have someone who cares so much and wants you to be happy, but all you do is run away from them. Well… I'm not running anymore."

Delilah kneeled in the dirt and took Iris's hand. All of the volunteers–even Marco–stopped what they were doing to watch.

"Iris, you accepted me for me. And that's the greatest gift anyone's ever given me in my entire life," said Delilah, choking on the words. "I'm sorry for pushing you away. And I'm sorry–" Delilah broke, having to take a moment to stop her crying and steady her breath. "I'm sorry if I let you down. That's the last thing in the world I ever wanted."

She kissed the top of Iris's hand and gazed up at her with teary eyes.

"I'm sorry too," said Iris. She knelt down with Delilah, Delilah inching her off the sidewalk and onto the garden's tilled soil. They laced their fingers together. "I said some awful things to you and I kept things from you I shouldn't have and I… I love you."

Delilah felt like her heart was about to burst.

"I love you too," she said back. It was the first time Delilah had uttered those words to anyone who wasn't family. She always thought saying them would make her as fragile as glass but now having spoken to them, Delilah felt invincible.

Iris looked around at the garden as she brushed a hand through her petaled hair; the petals seemed to rise at her touch, like flowers opening for the morning sun.

"This is unbelievable," she said. "We never would've gotten this much done on our own. How did you get all these people to help? And Marco? How did that happen?"

"I can tell you the gory boring details later," said Delilah. "But the lawsuit's off. All I had to do was what I thought my favorite green witch would've done.

"The lawsuit's off? That's fantastic!" exclaimed Iris. "And as for being a green witch… I think I'm, like, ready for a change. I don't think 'green witch' really suits me."

Delilah snorted a laugh and smiled. "What are you talking about?"

"I think I'm more of a city witch," said Iris.

"What's a city witch?" asked Delilah.

"Someone like, well, me. And maybe you, too. Though you can call yourself anything you want–as long as you're you."

"I was about to say the same thing to you, city witch," said Delilah.

Iris leaned forward and the witches kissed, ignoring the curious, gossiping onlookers. Someone whistled at them.

"By the way, I think you left your vines behind," Delilah said innocently. "Probably just a silly mistake after having to deal with a real mouthy, angry witch. But don't worry, they're okay– I've been taking care of them. Although…"

Iris's eyes widened. "What is it?"

"Don't be mad, okay? Remember the lily I, uh, gave you and then took back?"

"Uh huh…" Iris stiffened.

Delilah glanced away. "I'm not a green wi–" She caught herself. "I'm not great with plants and I think I may have, I don't know… do flowers ever suddenly dry out?"

Iris shook her head. She seemed suddenly anxious. Delilah decided they could talk about the lily later.

"Hey, I've been working on this garden all morning and I really could use a shower," she said with a grin. "Think you could give me a hand?"

They made it as far as Iris's room before they were wrestling on the carpet, their hands on one another's bodies, tearing off their clothes. A beam of sunlight fell on Delilah's naked alabaster body as Iris straddled her hips; Delilah resisted the urge to cover herself up, watching Iris watch her and savoring the happy look on the green–no, city–witch's face. It was going to take her some time to get used to that.

Iris lowered her head.

"I know I said I was sorry before," Iris said, looking down as she traced her fingers along Delilah's stomach. "But at the risk of bringing up old wounds, I just need to say–I really shouldn't have pushed you about your body. I'm okay if you want to be more, like, covered up or if you don't like the lights on or any stuff like that. I just was upset you didn't see you like I saw you, but that's not a good excuse. You can be any way you want to be and I'm still going to love you, okay?"

Hearing that declaration of love from Iris again made Delilah swell with joy. She cradled Iris's head in her hand, lifting her chin up so that the city witch could keep looking at her body. She nudged Iris back onto her heels and pulled herself up, standing so that Delilah's entire body was bathed in sunlight. She looked shyly down at Iris.

"I want to like the way I look as much as you do," she said, a lump in her throat. "I'm going to work on that–if you'll help me?"

Iris gave Delilah a teasing smile. "You know you can see into my room from the garden, right?"

Delilah realized she was putting on a show for the squad of volunteers and jumped out of the window's line of sight, throwing one arm around her chest and the other her crotch. Both women laughed.

"I'm glad you're here," said Delilah.

"There's nowhere else I'd rather be," Iris said.

Delilah stepped back into the sun, not caring if anyone was peeking inside. She held her hand out to Iris.

"Let's go take that shower."

~IRIS~

In the shower, they took turns exploring each other's body,

Delilah showing Iris how she liked to be touched and teased and licked and then letting Iris take over, giving into the petite witch's ministrations until she was nearly brought to her knees in a trembling, moaning orgasm. It made Iris feel on top of the world to be able to give the formidable witch such overwhelming pleasure. She was rewarded by Delilah's eager, greedy touch as Delilah practically shoved Iris against the shower wall and kissed her way from Iris's mouth down between her breasts and to the soft supple skin of her thighs. Then she worshipped Iris like she was drinking nectar from a sacred flower, holding her hand on Iris's stomach to feel every little motion.

"So, I have an idea," said Delilah while they got dressed in her room. Iris soaked up the sight of the tall, toned woman pulling on a pair of black high-waisted panties before she wriggled into her tight, torn denim jeans. As a topless Delilah searched through her clothes for a clean T-shirt, Iris slyly admired Delilah's pale bare breasts and her dark plum nipples.

Delilah explained how she had practiced her decompositions and the strange phantom sounds she heard from the chicken when she tried to reverse her magick.

"That sounds a lot like necromancy..." Iris warned, putting on a flowy, patterned maxi skirt and a crop top that left her shoulders exposed. "I'm not sure Arthur's kids–or Arthur, for that matter–want him to be raised from the dead."

Delilah sniffed at a crumpled-up tee, deciding it was still fresh enough to wear. "It's not necromancy. If it was, we'd be famous because it'd be the first act of necromancy anyone's ever performed."

"If it's not necromancy, what is it?" asked Iris, not convinced.

"I don't know, it felt more like... a memory or an echo from the past. I mean, it was only a piece of chicken so I'm not exactly sure what might happen with a person, but it didn't *feel* alive again, just that I heard what it sounded like when it had been alive," she explained as she put in her piercings and teased her hair into its fauxhawk shape.

Iris's petals needed far less maintenance. "But that's something that you felt because you're a, you know."

"You can say death witch, it's okay," said Delilah.

"Either way, even if you can 'hear' Arthur, how are you going to get his kids to hear him too?" asked Iris.

"Well, I was thinking that maybe we combine our magick. You're able to rouse plants, right? Get them to release compounds or whatever that affects people?"

Iris hmmed. "Combining magick... well it's not unheard of. Except there's one problem–Arthur's not a chicken breast. I don't think Arthur's kids are going to let us lop off a piece of him, assuming our magick even works together."

"I'm already two steps ahead of you," Delilah said proudly. She opened her bottommost drawer and took out something that was wrapped in a black garbage bag.

"Please tell me that's not Arthur."

Delilah chuckled. "Give me a little more credit than that, city witch. No, this is from the basement, where we got the gardening tools. Marco had a spare key, but there was a lot more down there than just tools."

Delilah opened the bag up and showed Iris what was inside. It looked like an old, sweat-stained baseball uniform, along with a cracked mitt and some mud-caked cleats. She cinched the bag shut again.

"It was his. Arthur's. He used to play, forever ago. It's not a piece of him but it sure looks pretty unwashed to me," she said. "I'm sure *some* of him is still stuck to it."

Iris wrinkled her nose at the thought that the uniform hadn't been washed for decades. "Will it work?" she asked.

"There's only one way to find out," said Delilah.

Back in the garden, Iris was once again stunned at how much Delilah, Marco, and the other tenants had done in such a short time. The planting was wholly unlike what Iris had planned, and she could feel a kaleidoscope clash of flower and plant auras nestled in the ground, along with the one corner where she had placed her own plants–and set Vin down so that he could enjoy the outdoors. But despite the chaos of the seed planting, there was also something unexpectedly harmonious about it.

That wasn't the only harmony to be found in the garden. Iris watched as Delilah and Marco spoke, the two showing each other a respect that would've been unthinkable a week and a half ago.

"Just a circle in the middle of the garden?" asked Marco. "Like a centerpiece?"

"More like a memorial," said Delilah. "For Arthur. Nothing

huge, just enough room for a few flowers. After we've planted them, I was thinking we could have his kids come by to see it."

"Do you think they'll be okay with that?" Iris asked Marco.

It was the first words she'd exchanged with Marco since the day of the fire. The guilt was still on his face, hidden in the creases of his forehead and crow's feet by his eyes.

"Hmmm. They were very close and didn't expect him to go so soon," said Marco. "It'll be tough to get them down here. But I'll do my best. Although, why do I feel like there's something you're not telling me?"

"We do have a surprise for them," said Iris.

Delilah whipped her head around to give Iris a chastising look.

"It's okay," Iris said to her. Then she turned back to Marco. "It's a good surprise, not a bad one. Trust us."

Marco leaned on the garden spade he had stuck into the dirt. He sighed. "Alright. Consider yourselves trusted, lovebirds."

Death & Life

~IRIS~

Although Marco was able to convince Jacob and Andrea–or Jake and Andi, as they preferred to be called–to visit the sprouting community garden, he made sure the witches knew it was no easy feat; Arthur's kids were still raw and grieving. The visit was set for five days before the eviction deadline. A handful of tenants had left the building already, but the rest seemed to be holding their breath–amazingly, their one-time fear and hatred of the witches in 1B had turned into hope that these strange young women had an ace up their sleeves that would save the day.

Iris wanted to share their hope but was struggling. She and Delilah had tried to combine Iris's green magick with Delilah's reverse-decay trick a dozen times, but something always went wrong–the practice meat decayed or the plant withered or its flower buds released noxious compounds that sent Iris and Delilah rushing out of their apartment.

At least they were able to spend their last days in Unit 1B together. It wasn't all cuddles in bed and steamy showers, although there were plenty of both. The witches also found new ways to play together. Iris's favorite new game was "Dress Up", where the witches would take turns picking outfits for each other and doing one another's makeup, letting Iris eagerly teach Delilah all her glow-up secrets. One time she had Delilah in nothing but a midriff-exposing camo hoodie with the sleeves cut off and a pair of low-rise stretch denim jeans that showed the straps of the V-string she wore underneath, Iris's makeup job giving Delilah exotic, smoky eyes and pink-black ombre lips. Admiring how Delilah's twin raven tattoo on her shoulder went with the outfit, she was reminded once again of her strange experience in the woods of Cold Spring.

"I never told you where I went," she said to Delilah as the other witch checked herself out in the mirror, seeming more confident in her body by the day.

Delilah frowned. "I was curious but after the last time, with Times Square, I didn't want to pry," she said.

Iris told her about the woods and how the trees had called her an outsider. Then she told her about the dreams she had, leading all the way up to the not-Delilah woman with the ravens on her shoulders. When Iris was done, Delilah stood there with an unsettled look on her face.

"Are you sure that happened?" she asked as kindly as she could. "Memory can be a funny thing. You said yourself you didn't remember a few things that happened there. Maybe the stress of everything going on affected you?"

"I'm positive that's what happened," said Iris.

Delilah furrowed her brow.

"What is it?" Iris asked.

"I don't wanna freak you out, but the woman you described with the silvery eyes… that sounds a lot like how Abaddon's supposed to look. You know who that is, right?"

Iris's throat felt very dry. "It's who some death witches pray to, right?"

Delilah nodded. "And the lily, well, I actually got you a calla lily because I saw online it means rebirth. I wanted it to be for us, you know? I mean, the way we were together after barely talking this past year. But then when I gave it to you, I felt dumb telling a green witch what a flower was supposed to mean, especially when you didn't seem all too impressed by it."

"Sorry about that," said Iris, glancing away. "But what are you getting at? That the woman I dreamt of was Abaddon? And that she 'took' the lily to… what? Let me out of the woods?"

"To let you live," said Delilah. She was truly spooked now. "Maybe she took it as an offering or something."

"Does that happen?"

Delilah shook her head. "I have no idea."

The day of Jake and Andi's visit was there before the witches knew it. They prepared the night before, burying Arthur's old baseball uniform in the memorial circle Marco and the other tenants had built out, covering it with fresh mulch and, inspired by Iris's dream in the Cold Spring woods, planting a bundle of white calla lilies on top.

Neither witch was able to sleep much, thanks to the unseasonably hot spring night. They stayed in Iris's room, surrounded by her vines with their naked bodies sprawled out on the bed. Iris was grateful to be able to touch Delilah's cool, pale skin and rested her head on the witch's chest while Delilah stroked her petaled hair. Now that they were no longer smothered by the pink wig, those petals seemed to grow every day, some starting to bloom into full pink flowers.

"Are you nervous about tomorrow?" asked Iris.

"Yes. No. I don't know," said Delilah.

"That covers all the options," teased Iris.

Delilah squeezed Iris's side, making her laugh and squirm.

"If I seem distracted, it's because there was something I was supposed to do," Delilah said once Iris's laughter calmed down. "For that job I told you I had. They paid me in advance."

"And you didn't do it?" asked Iris.

"I couldn't. I tried, but…" Delilah sighed.

"It wasn't you."

Delilah smiled and pulled Iris close. Iris nudged her nose against the crook of Delilah's armpit, enjoying her rich, unadulterated scent. She wished she could stay that way, not asking the questions that lingered in her mind.

"Aren't they going to want their money back?" asked Iris.

"Probably," Delilah said.

"What are you going to do?"

"I don't know. I've spent a big chunk of it already. And if we have to leave this building, I'll have to spend more of it."

"Delilah…"

"I guess that just means we need to pull off this little magick trick tomorrow," said Delilah. "So that we can stay, along with everyone else."

Iris huffed a laugh. "No pressure."

"I believe in you," Delilah said. She kissed Iris on the top of her head, between her silky petals. Iris had never been happier to be without her wig.

"I believe in you too," Iris said back.

Iris's hand searched for Delilah's, their fingers intertwining. She slowly drifted off into a deep and dreamless sleep.

~DELILAH~

Nearly everyone who was left in the building on Madison Street came down for Jake and Andi's visit to the community garden. Compared to a week ago, the lot was unrecognizable, Iris having used her green magick to speed up the growth of the planted seeds. The result was a flourishing sprawl of foliage of all colors, shapes, and scents that was already attracting curious pollinators. Throughout the greenery, Marco had created a meandering pathway that branched off to peaceful nooks where refurbished benches sat; he'd also marked off empty plots where he was already planning to replant saplings promised to them by GreenThumb. In the center of the garden was a raised circle made of segmented, polished stone, filled with fresh earth, a half-dozen white calla lilies and–known only to the witches– Arthur's old baseball uniform.

When Jake and Andi finally arrived, they looked overwhelmed to see so many people there to greet them, the pair dressed in chic West Village fashion that suggested that whatever life their father lived, it had paved the way for their own largess.

"Marco, hi," said Jake, giving the older man a firm, confident handshake. Jake looked around at the tenants, waving to a few though looking like he couldn't quite remember who they were. As his sweeping gaze reached Delilah and Iris, he paused.

Seeing Jake and Andi's confusion, Marco stepped in.

"Jake, Andi–these are some of our newer tenants, Delilah and Iris."

The witches shook hands with Arthur's kids.

"Iris…" said Andi. "You were the one who emailed us about Dad."

"Oh yeah," said Jake.

Andi tilted her head to the side. "I didn't realize you were, um…" She pointed at Delilah and then Iris. "Paras? Can I say that? And I think… witches?"

"I thought Dad had to keep this building para-free to extend out the 421-a benefits…" said Jake.

Jake's comment caught Marco off guard. Delilah's heart skipped a beat. Was their plan about to backfire?

"You know how your dad was," Marco was quick to say. "He always bent the rules to do what was right. These two are as blue collar as it comes–a bartender and… what was it again?"

"She works at the Strand," Delilah said, knowing Iris had quit her job but hoping it wouldn't matter.

Andi nodded approvingly. "I love the Strand," she said.

Jake looked less impressed. He put his hands on his hips. "I don't want to be rude Marco, but even just seeing Dad's building over there is making this hard for me. I'm touched you guys made a memorial, but would you mind if we got on with it?"

"Oh sure, sure!" said Marco. He looked back at Delilah and Iris as he ushered Jake and Andi towards the calla lilies, a concerned look on his face.

Iris stood up on her tippy-toes and whispered into Delilah's ear: "You've got this. Remember, I love you."

Delilah mouthed the words back to Iris.

The witches followed behind Marco, and when Jake and Andi reached the memorial, they stepped around to make sure they were close to the lilies and the buried uniform.

"It's beautiful," said Andi. She was tearing up.

Jake scratched his head. "I don't think Dad was ever into flowers–"

"Jake! That's not the point!" said Andi, scolding her brother. "Callas are all about resurrection. I saw it in *Vogue*. What a beautiful choice."

Delilah had to try hard not to smile, pleased that someone else knew the lily's significance.

"Relax, I don't read *Vogue*, okay?" murmured Jake. He knelt down, not caring that his light slacks were touching the dirt speckled flagstone path, and touched his hand to the fresh earth. "That's funny…"

"What?" asked Andi.

"Get down here, smell this," he said, scooping up a tiny handful of the dirt for his sister. "Doesn't it smell like Dad?"

Andi bent down towards the dirt and sniffed. "Oh yeah, it

kind of does. Weird."

Delilah quietly took Iris's hand and squeezed. It was time.

She did as they'd rehearsed, the two witches focusing on the calla lilies and the buried uniform, Delilah "pulling her punch" with as much focus and strength as she could muster. For some reason, Iris's dream popped into her head, and Delilah imagined the silvery-eyed woman Iris had described who bore a striking resemblance to Abaddon.

I've never really thought you were real, but I sure wouldn't mind being wrong right about now....

But nothing happened.

Jake stood up, dusting off his slacks. "This was sweet Marco, really," he said. He looked at Iris. "And between this and your email, I know what you guys were hoping for, I really do. I wish Dad could've stayed with us and we could've figured all of this out at not such short notice."

Delilah's stomach sank.

Andi nodded as her brother spoke. "Totally agreed. I am so touched at what you did for Dad and I think this entire garden is just gorgeous. I wish he were here to see it."

"Maybe in another life," said Jake, wistfully. "I think he would have really liked it."

"Liked it?" said an ethereal, warbly voice. "I would've loved it, Jakey."

The siblings shot each other a shocked look and the tenants looked around, perplexed. Delilah could feel Iris looking at her but her own eyes were locked on the calla lilies as a chill ran through her.

"What is this?" asked Jake. He looked up at Delilah accusingly. "Some kind of black magic?"

"I… I honestly don't know," said Delilah.

Jake's expression hardened. "Like hell you don't," he said.

"Jake, calm down," said Marco, although his look to Delilah suggested he was also upset by what was happening.

"I'm not going to calm down!" shouted Jake. He glared at Delilah. "Did you think you could just impersonate my father and we'd just decide not to sell the building? Are you insane?"

"Jakey, I didn't raise you to be a butthead," the Arthur-voice said.

A fog rose up from the dirt of the memorial taking on the

vague shape of a person. The onlooking tenants gasped and even Iris grabbed Delilah's hand tightly.

Holy shit, thought Delilah. *What the hell did we just do?*

Jake laughed despite his anger and turned to Andi. "Did he say butthead?"

"That was Dad's thing," Andi said. "Remember? We used to laugh at him for it. He never wanted to curse in front of us."

"How are you doing this?" Jake asked Delilah. "I demand you tell me."

"Pfft! Andi, can you tell your brother to be quiet and listen?" said the Arthur-voice. "Just like always, the little old man is talking over me."

That got both of the siblings to look towards the amorphous form that had taken shape above the callas.

Delilah jumped in while the kids stared at the misty cloud. "Listen, we were trying to do something for you, but it was just to give you a flash of memory of your dad, just a little something to remember him by. But this... I don't know what this is. It's more... it's stronger than I thought it'd be."

The Arthur-voice laughed warmly. "I wish I had something better to tell you kids but it feels like I was calling you and the operator just connected us. Dunno a better way to put it. But I don't think the connection will last long. Let's not waste the time we have."

Everyone was quiet then, giving the Arthur-voice room to speak.

"Andi, Jakey... I'm sorry I left so suddenly," the Arthur-voice said. "There was so much more I wanted to say to you and so much more of your lives I wanted to see."

Both Jake and Andi started crying, looking up at the misty cloud with heartbreak in their eyes.

"If you take nothing else from this moment, know that I loved you both so, so much. You were the light of me and your mother's lives and no matter if things were easy or hard or friggin' impossible, I never regretted a single moment with the two of you. Even when you broke my turntable–I know that was you by the way, Andi."

Jake's eyes went wide. "I knew it!"

Andi cry-laughed and smiled at her brother. "Oops."

"And did I hear that right? You're selling my building?" asked the Arthur-voice.

The kids hushed up.

"Like hell you are," the Arthur-voice said. "Do you think I took care of that building for fifty years so the two of you could sell it the second I died?"

"But Dad…" started Jake.

"Jakey."

"It's ancient," continued Jake. "There's a ton of overdue maintenance. There are ten developers who will give us *double* the assessed value without us having to lift a finger." Seeing that his sister wasn't as adamant as he was, Jake changed his tact: "How do we even know what you're saying is real? What if these witches are just manipulating your words?"

The Arthur-voice was ominously quiet. When it spoke again, there was a smile in its voice.

"You've always been a skeptical boy, Jakey. It's not a bad trait. You want proof of what I'm saying? Go to my study in Elmhurst and check the red notebook. It's a mess, but I was trying to get my thoughts together for you and Andi before, you know… this happened."

Jake opened his mouth to speak and the Arthur-voice cut him off.

"You sell that building to a developer and the only people who will be able to afford to live in whatever they build will be the rich nudniks. Is that what you want? For no normal person to have a place to live?"

Jake and Andi said in unison: "No, Dad."

"Good, then that's enough of that," the Arthur-voice said. "Oh, is that Marco there? Hey Marco."

"Hey Artie," said Marco, a sad smile on his face. "They got Bud in heaven?"

The Arthur-voice laughed. "Just Heineken."

"Christ," said Marco, joining the Arthur-voice in his laughter.

"I don't think I have much time left," said the Arthur-voice. "Can I have some time alone with my kids, please?"

Delilah, Iris, Marco, and the rest of the tenants split off, walking along the flagstone paths to the bench books and edges of the garden. Delilah's mind reeled as she tried to understand what she had just witnessed. Was that her and Iris's magick? Had they really connected with Arthur on the other side?

When she and Iris reached the iron wrought fence, Delilah saw a familiar face staring at her from the other side.

"Can I help you?" asked Iris.

Ralph Ellison smirked. "The two of you seem nice together," he said. "You must be Iris."

Iris looked anxiously at Delilah.

"Ralph, I was just about to text y–"

"Calm down. I'm not here on bad terms. I see you didn't do the job I requested…"

Delilah saw Ralph looking past her at Marco as he continued to usher tenants away from the community garden memorial.

"…but it seems like you won him over in your own way," said Ralph.

Ignoring Iris's growing confusion, Delilah said: "I can pay you back if you want."

Ralph waived away her worry. "Keep it. It's not much anyway. But Ms. Cruz, I would like you to consider what we talked about. I'm not upset you seem to have influenced Mr. Galeano, but you can't influence millions of New Yorkers. There may be a moment when something more is required."

"Something more like what?" asked Iris.

As Ralph looked at Iris, there seemed to be something else in the gleam of his eye than his usual cool, calculating stare. He nodded to himself.

"You two *are* good for each other," he said.

Then, in the blink of an eye, Ralph Ellison was gone.

"Who was that?" asked Iris.

"The Invisible Man," said Delilah.

~IRIS~

Anyway Bar was slammed for 3 p.m. on a Tuesday. But the crowd wasn't all witches today, a throng of older neighborhood folk taking over the bar to celebrate that they no longer had to find new places to live.

Ruth was chatting with Marco, the two of them talking tattoos and Marco going on and on about how he was their building's new super, the endless conversation driving the other tenants away to try their hand at the jukebox. Soon Anyway Bar was filled with 70s and 80s hits that got half the bar dancing in no time.

Iris and Delilah were perched on the dark side of the bar, sipping on whiskies neither intended to finish; there were far more fun things to do than get drunk.

"What do you think?" asked Iris.

"A job for you at the Parks Department? Do you really think that's the right fit for a city witch? Sounds more like green witch work to me," teased Delilah.

Iris rolled her eyes. "You're never going to let that go, are you?"

"Like you would want me to," replied Delilah, poking Iris in the side playfully. "I think it's the perfect job for you. Just make sure you don't trim these."

Delilah ran her hand through the bed of satiny pink roses crowning Iris's head, the feel of her brushing palm sending an electric pulse down Iris's spine that made her swoon.

Iris blushed. She loved when Delilah touched her flower hair and had to keep herself from getting too excited.

"How about yourself?" asked Iris. "Would the venerable Delilah Cruz ever leave the bartender-thrift-store life? I'm sure you could do a lot of good with the Parks Department."

Delilah nodded slowly. "I'm sure I could," she said without a trace of irony or hubris. "But for the first time in a long, long time, I'm happy where I am. And why fix what isn't broken?"

"I know exactly what you mean."

THE END

Thank You!

Thank you so much for reading *Two Broke Witches*! Want more of Iris and Delilah? Check out the prequel short story *Witchmates*, available for free by signing up for my Starling's Darlings newsletter, where you'll receive updates from me, special offers, and calls to participate in beta reading and ARC reviews. Just head over to sendfox.com/katestarlingwrites to sign up and read *Witchmates* right away!

One last note: reviews are vitally important for indie authors like myself and help provide the needed social proof that helps sell more books. If you aren't too busy and can leave a review on the store you bought or read *Two Broke Witches* from, I'd be incredibly grateful! Thank you!

About the Author

Hi, I'm Kate Starling! I write Sapphic fantasy romance and my mision (well, one of them) is to showcase realistic characters in fantastical settings with a juicy splash of spice and smut to keep things exciting. When I'm not writing romance, you can find me reading (of course), checking out new restaurants, and pedaling away on my Peloton. Oh, and spending time with my furbabies too! I was born and raised in New York, but I love adventuring to new places and meeting people from different walks of life.

Printed in Great Britain
by Amazon